Margi McAllister
FAWN

SCHOLASTIC

First published in the UK in 2013 by Scholastic Children's Books
An imprint of Scholastic Ltd
Euston House, 24 Eversholt Street
London, NW1 1DB, UK
Registered office: Westfield Road, Southam, Warwickshire, CV47 0RA
SCHOLASTIC and associated logos are trademarks
and/or registered trademarks of Scholastic Inc.

Text copyright © Margaret McAllister, 2013

The right of Margaret McAllister to be identified as
the author of this work has been asserted by her.

The Fell Types are digitally reproduced by Igino Marini.

ISBN 978 1 407 13105 4

A CIP catalogue record for this book
is available from the British Library.

Printed and bound by CPI Group (UK) Ltd, Croydon, CR0 4YY
Papers used by Scholastic Children's Books are made from
wood grown in sustainable forests.

1 3 5 7 9 10 8 6 4 2

This is a work of fiction. Names, characters, places, incidents and dialogues are
products of the author's imagination or are used fictitiously. Any resemblance to
actual people, living or dead, events or locales is entirely coincidental.

www.scholastic.co.uk/zone
www.margaretmcallister.co.uk

FAWN

To Jo, with love

Chapter One

If there was one child in the school who seemed different from the others, it was Kirsty Weaver.

What was it about Kirsty? She didn't show off, or make trouble, or do anything to make people notice her. She was quiet, and a bit daydreamy. Maybe it was the way she always came to school looking as if she'd been thrown together in a hurry, with her hair scraped back into an elastic band and her shoes badly scuffed around the toes. Her uniform was usually clean but it always needed ironing, or at least a good straightening up and smoothing down. She often seemed to have her mind on something else, as if school wasn't all that important.

Nobody at school knew much about Kirsty. On this particular May morning, before school, they wouldn't have guessed where she was. Kirsty liked it that way. She preferred to go unnoticed. She liked the freedom of being on her own. Some things were too special to tell everyone about.

People often said Kirsty lived in a world of her own. Kirsty actually felt as if she lived in three very different worlds. Each one had its own colours, like a painter's palette.

School was a world of bright colours and loud voices, where they called you names if you had the wrong sweater on, and it was important to avoid Georgia Wilkinson and Sally Cook, who would pick on her if they felt like it. Displays on the school walls were in bold, strong shades as if everything had to be clear and simple.

Home just now was grey, with Mum always sad and tired, as if she was dragging a heavy weight around with her. Mum never laughed any more, or even really smiled. She was limp, like a burst balloon. The house was always dim and dusty and a bit of a mess, but Dad didn't notice and Kirsty tried not to. But she didn't want to think about that now.

The world Kirsty was in now was her favourite. This was her green world, full of so many different greens. She was standing in the hushed, leafy wood high in the hills above her house. This wood belonged to the rabbits, the foxes and the night owls, but most of all to the deer. With their proud antlers, graceful walk and white spotted backs, the fallow deer ruled this hill. Its trees and its clearings were theirs, and watching them was Kirsty's favourite way to start the day.

 2

The best place for seeing the deer was reached by a long, steep climb up the hill and a twisting, sometimes muddy path through the trees to the heart of the wood. On a bright morning like this, early sunshine filtered through the leaves and scattered patterns across the grass, but the air was still cool. Silent as a ghost, Kirsty pulled her worn-out old coat round her for warmth and settled down on an old, rather damp tree trunk to watch.

The deer blended into the background so well that if she hadn't known what to look for, Kirsty might not have seen them. A pale limb could be a thin young tree trunk. Were those branches among the oak trees, or antlers? But Kirsty was practised at this, and watched patiently for movement. Shadows shifted. Branches rustled. Yes, the herd had gathered here, half-hidden among the trees.

A spiky shape moved, swayed, and dipped. Not a branch, but the head and broad antlers of a fully grown stag. Kirsty could make out the shape of his long, slender legs stepping towards her between the trees, and the pale gleam of his chest. He lowered his head to graze, pulling leaves into his mouth, then walked away, deeper into the wood.

The whole day ahead of Kirsty looked better now that she had seen the stag so clearly. She smiled, and wriggled a bit – it was time to make her way quietly back down the hill – but what happened next was so astonishing and so perfect that she could scarcely breathe.

3

A dappled deer with the smooth head of a female crossed the clearing and walked slowly into the deep cover of bracken and young heather. Often, she stopped to twist herself round and lick at her tail. Kirsty leaned forward to watch her more closely. This doe had the same white spots as all fallow deer, but one ear was darker than the other and there was a still-healing patch on her leg where she must have grazed it. Steadily, not rushing, the doe walked on, further from the herd, stopping now and again to turn and lick. This wasn't a deer wandering about the hill, foraging for food. She had a sense of purpose and was looking for exactly the right place, and Kirsty knew why. There was only one reason a doe would keep cleaning herself like that. She was about to give birth.

She would soon be out of sight. Kirsty stood up very slowly, knowing that any sudden movement would alarm the doe, and slipped silently through the trees to the rising ground. She knew a good viewpoint where the rocky hillside made a rough hollow, a perfect place for looking down into the forest. She climbed up and sat there, watching intently for any movement.

The doe stopped under the shelter of a silver birch tree and waited, calm and patient, still cleaning round her tail. A shaft of bright sunlight fell on her back. Then, as Kirsty barely breathed, something wet and shiny slithered to the ground at the deer's feet. Something with hooves and a tiny head.

Kirsty had grown up under the shelter of this hill and there had always been a deer herd. She had seen young

4

ones close to their mothers, and she had heard stags bellowing and fighting in the autumn when it was too dangerous to go near them, but she had never before seen a birth. Her throat tightened, and she rubbed her eyes quickly. If they filled with tears she wouldn't be able to see clearly, and she mustn't miss any of this.

The doe lay down at last, nuzzling the tiny, shiny fawn lying beside her, and never stopped licking it until it was clean and dry. Even at a distance Kirsty could just make out the shape of it, its damp dark back and its brave, wobbling attempts to stand up.

Now that the fawn was clean, the neat little pattern of white spots on its back was clear. It was so perfect, Kirsty found she was biting her lip and holding her breath as she watched, wanting to see every detail of the small head and the tiny hooves. Even blinking would be too much. In all her life, she had never seen anything so lovely as this fawn.

Oh, Mum, thought Kirsty. *You should be here. Surely you wouldn't be so sad if you could be here. If only Auntie Sarah could be here, too, then we could all watch it together.*

Kirsty had learned a lot about deer from books and websites as well as from watching them with her aunt, and she knew what the mother would do next. As soon as the fawn could walk, she'd lead it away to a safe place and leave it there. She wouldn't abandon it – she'd go back to feed and clean it – but it would be safer alone, hidden from anything that might harm it. A full-grown female deer could easily be seen, but a baby

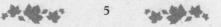

lying in the undergrowth would be safe. Kirsty hoped he wouldn't mind being alone. Now that she thought about it, her mum was a bit like a deer mum, too. A mum who didn't fuss over her. *And that's fine with me*, thought Kirsty. *I'm not the one who needs looking after.*

Unfortunately, Kirsty couldn't stay here all morning. She had to go to school. School was the world of bright colours, but it seemed to cast a shadow over her morning.

There were some things Kirsty loved about school. Like everyone else, she had some favourite lessons. She enjoyed any lesson that could take her imagination to different times and places, and got bored by anything to do with graphs, calculations or how electricity worked. Being a girl who loved animals, she liked environmental studies, but as she generally knew more about it than anyone else in the class, including the teacher, she could get bored with that, too. (And she had learned long ago not to let anyone see how much she knew. It was hard enough being a misfit without being a know-it-all, too.)

School wouldn't be so bad, though, if only *they* would leave her alone. It was the kind of bullying she couldn't explain to a teacher. Sally and Georgia didn't steal her dinner money or wait around corners to beat her up. There was just the hair-tweaking, the whispered name-calling, the tripping up, the mimicking of her voice. On top of that was the innocent way that they would say "Nice shoes, Kirsty," so that other people would look and see that her shoes were scuffed or muddy or worn out. Or "Have you just had your hair done?" so everyone would notice that it hadn't been washed for a week, let alone cut.

Kirsty sighed. It was hard, very hard, to leave the hill. More than ever, it felt like an enchanted wood in a story, and she wanted so much to stay. But this wasn't an enchanted wood. At the bottom of the hill was her house and her dad's garage. And on the other side of the house was a long grey road, where the bus would come to carry her off to school.

Keeping every movement slow and smooth, she stood up and slipped away, turning for one last glance at the mother and her baby. The doe nuzzled it as it wobbled on its spindly legs, trying to suckle.

As she walked downhill, Kirsty wondered what her life might be like if this really was an enchanted wood. There'd be no room for Georgia and Sally in it, or at least, not unless they got lost, and were chased by wolves and fell over a cliff. It would be a perfect world, where Mum would be fine, and laugh, and be like a normal mum, and Auntie Sarah wouldn't have died. But today, on the stony, muddy path, not even those thoughts could make Kirsty sad. She had seen the birth of a fawn. She went over every moment in her memory, seeing again the soft, elegant head of the doe as she licked her baby, its neat hooves and its tiny mottled back. By the time Kirsty was nearly home, that image had settled in her heart like a scene in a snow globe.

The valley was spread before her like a toy town. The long grey road made it a good place for Dad's

work, which was repairing cars. The low wooden fence that separated the woodland from the yard and the garage forecourt was like a border between the green world and the grey one, but the trees and bushes grew through it, refusing to be kept out.

Beside the garage was a heap of old tyres and a car balanced on four bricks. That car had been there for as long as Kirsty could remember, and as it had lost its bonnet and Dad had emptied the engine for spare parts, she supposed it would stay there until something built a nest in it or it dropped to bits, whichever happened first. The tiny garage office faced the house and there was just room for a shop where Dad sold things that drivers might need, like car stuff and Mars Bars. They used to sell groceries, cards, flowers and pot plants, but that had been in the days when Mum had been well enough to help.

On the other side of the yard, as far away from the house as it could be without falling over the fence, was a shed. They used to have all sorts of plans for that shed. For years they had talked about turning it into a shop, or a tearoom, or a studio where Mum could paint and sell her pictures. But Mum hadn't thought her pictures were good enough, and she never painted now, and it would cost too much money to repair the shed anyway. So it stayed unchanged, divided into a row of horse stalls along one side, with mangers still fastened to the wall. It was big enough to have a party in, and one day there might be something to have a party about. You never knew. Meanwhile, the black paint on the door was peeling off.

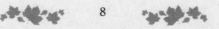

And there, between the garage on one side and the shed on the other, with its back to the road, was their house, like a big grey box with a roof. Round the front door, a few dried-up plants in flowerpots trailed out across the yard as if they'd been trying to escape and had died in the attempt. Nobody took care of them any longer, but this morning there were bluebells on the hill, so Kirsty had picked some of those for Mum on the way down.

She looked across to the deeply wooded hillside on the other side of the road. Hart Hill Farm was up there, almost hidden in the trees, but it wasn't a real farm any more. Toby Gordon, who was in Kirsty's class, lived there. His parents weren't farmers – they were a bit posh and worked at something to do with the law – but they lived in a farmhouse and kept sheep. Goodness only knew why, but they did. The Gordons had invited Kirsty up there at lambing time and she'd loved seeing the new lambs all wet and slippery from birth. They were sweet and a bit disgusting at the same time. Walking down the hill, still thinking about the fawn, Kirsty wondered if all newborn things were like that, wet and messy and helpless, and completely lovable.

Toby and his family hadn't lived there very long, so Toby had come into the class later than everyone else, and had had to start from the beginning with fitting in and making friends. Being brainy and a bit geeky hadn't helped, so Kirsty had looked out for him until he seemed able to look out for himself. Somebody had to.

Thinking about Toby reminded Kirsty that she'd

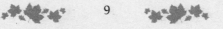

have to be on the school bus soon. But she'd be home before four and could go deer-watching again as soon as she'd changed out of her uniform and checked if Mum needed anything. That was something to look forward to.

Sometimes Kirsty felt that her own family was like a deer family, but she was the mother, watching over the one who was helpless. She was so used to it that she hardly thought about it any longer. She just got on with looking after Mum, cooking dinner, loading the dishwasher, putting the dishes away, doing the washing, keeping things going.

That day at Hart Hill Farm, watching the lambing, had been the last time anything bright had happened in Kirsty's life until today. Now that she had seen the birth of the fawn, a voice inside her longed to tell everyone about it. But that was a young voice, a childish voice, and Kirsty decided not to listen to it. The older voice in Kirsty said – *Be careful. Do what the mother's doing. Keep quiet.*

It looked as if it might rain, so she thought she'd better wear her coat to school. It was a padded anorak, old, blue and faded, and one day Kirsty might even get round to sewing the toggles back on, but it was warm and comfortable, and it only took a good shake to get the bits of moss and twig off it. As she came through the gate which marked the end of the wood and the beginning of home, Dad was already outside the garage in his oily jeans and old jacket. (She often wondered if Dad knew that there was a little round patch on

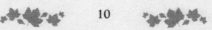

10

the top of his head where his sandy hair was so thin, it was almost a bald spot. She never mentioned it, in case he hadn't noticed.) This morning he was talking to Mal, and Mal – oh, he was just Mal, with big boots and tattoos on his arms. He wasn't old or young. He did a bit of work for Dad – in fact, everything Mal did seemed to be "a bit of work". He did a bit of work at Hart Hill Farm, mostly at lambing time. Apart from working for Dad, he also did a bit of gardening, a bit of hammering and mending, a bit of taxi driving and a bit of gravedigging for the church when necessary. She could hear them talking about engines and tyre pressures and power steering, which made no sense at all to her.

"Off to school today, Kirsty?" asked Mal. That was what really irritated her about him. If something was too obvious to be said, he'd say it.

"I went up the hill first," she said. "I got Mum some flowers." Dad nodded as if he approved.

"Did you see them deer up there?" asked Mal, but Kirsty only nodded and shrugged as if she couldn't care less about the deer. They were all too precious and beautiful to be talked about here, to Mal and Dad, who wouldn't understand how she felt about them. That would spoil the magic. She turned to go, but Mal went on.

"They look nice enough, but they're a nuisance, them deer. Come the autumn they get dangerous. You don't want to go up there in the autumn when the stags are bellowing, right?"

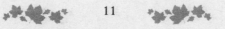

"I know," said Kirsty politely. *It's called the rut and I know all about it*, she thought.

"And all the rest of the year they're chewing the bark off the trees," continued Mal relentlessly. "Them young saplings don't get a chance with the deer chewing on them. I've lost rows and rows of young trees to them deer. Shall I tell you the best thing for a deer?"

Kirsty didn't answer. He'd tell her anyway.

"A gun," said Mal, and Dad laughed. "One shot to the head, and there's a nice bit of venison. Lovely."

Kirsty pictured the new fawn nuzzling, seeking his mother's warm milk. The mention of a gun made her feel sick. Mal turned to Dad.

"Ever had venison, Andy?" he asked.

"I have," said Dad. "It's very good."

"It needs red wine gravy," said Mal firmly. "And little new potatoes. Beautiful. Beautiful. You know the people at Hart Hill Farm, don't you, Kirsty?"

"A bit," she said. "I've been there."

"I was up there yesterday," he said. "I had a look at the lambs for 'em. The first of them lambs will be ready to go for slaughter next week. First of the spring lamb. Lovely."

Isn't it more lovely while it's still running around on its four legs? wondered Kirsty crossly as she walked to the house, fishing through the hole in her pocket for the key. Indoors, the familiar house smell met her – a whiff of washing powder, and the sour taint of clothes that had been left drying around the house for too long, turning damp and a bit pongy. She made a cup of tea the way Mum liked it, and found the prettiest vase she could for the bluebells.

Kirsty tapped at the door and went in without waiting for an answer, as Mum might still be asleep. In the sleep-smelling bedroom the light was dim, and Mum turned her head drowsily towards her. At least she was awake, even if she wasn't up. Sometimes she stayed in bed all day.

"Cup of tea, Mum," said Kirsty brightly, "and some bluebells, look!"

Mum sat up slowly, as if it hurt her to move. Her hair, dark red like Kirsty's, was tousled and needed a wash and there were shadows around her eyes, but she managed a weak smile as she reached out a hand for the flowers.

"Beautiful bluebells," she murmured, as if every word was a struggle. Kirsty spread out some clothes over a chair in the hope of encouraging Mum to get up and dressed, but Mum hadn't cared much about clothes, or food either, since the depression had taken hold. Kirsty imagined depression as a great grey shapeless mouth that ate you from the inside out. She pulled open the curtains, and against the faded duvet cover and dull wallpaper, the bluebells brightened the room.

"Tell Dad to put some washing in," whispered Mum.

"I've done the washing," said Kirsty. She'd had to, otherwise she wouldn't have had a clean shirt today. It was funny that Dad was so brilliant with engines but he couldn't handle a washing machine. If there were three

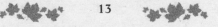 13

things to do – *turn the first dial, turn the second dial, press the button* – he'd forget one of them.

Mum held out her hand to Kirsty. "I'm a rubbish mother," she said in a low, tired voice. "I'm so sorry."

Kirsty hugged her. "You're a great mother," she told her. "And you're getting better. You were up most of yesterday evening. Wasn't it good, curling up on the settee together? Eating toast and watching telly? We should do that more often, Mum. See you later. Love you loads."

Yesterday had been encouraging, and Kirsty was hoping for another good day. It was time to go to school now and leave Mum for the day, like the mother deer leaving the baby.

"Off to the bus, then?" Mal called after her as she made the short walk to the bus stop. Toby from Hart Hill Farm was waiting there, too. Short, neat and tidy Toby with his jet black hair and glasses. He was always a bit awkward and shy and never said much.

Perhaps this will be one of the better days too, thought Kirsty, and yawned. Two good days in a row. Was that too much to hope for?

Chapter Two

"Kirsty!"

She jerked. The class giggled.

"Kirsty?" repeated Mrs Baines.

Kirsty was sitting at her desk in the classroom but her mind was on the hill, looking down at the fawn. All morning she had wondered about it, and whether its mother had found it a safe place yet, and was it afraid? Was it warm enough? It was only the size of a small dog, and there were always foxes about. She imagined a circle of protection round it, keeping harm away, but she could only imagine it. She couldn't really do anything to protect the fawn. It was only when Mrs Baines, her class teacher, suddenly said her name that her mind came back to the classroom.

Apparently Mrs Baines had just asked a question,

but she had no idea what it was. Her face felt red and hot, and she tried to guess what Mrs Baines had been talking about. She curled her toes in her shoes as Sally and Georgia turned to glare at her, grinning like pumpkin lanterns. Across the table, Toby Gordon was scrawling something on the back of his hand.

"I know it's Monday, Kirsty, but try to stay awake," said Mrs Baines. "Did you hear the question?"

There was more giggling, but Mrs Baines stopped it with a glare, then turned her attention back to Kirsty. Toby's hand was on the table, turned a little towards Kirsty, but she couldn't see it clearly.

"If you had no central heating, no gas, and no electricity," said Mrs Baines, "what would you use for fuel?"

That was easy. "Coal," said Kirsty. "Or wood."

"Thank you," said Mrs Baines, and went on with the lesson, which was something to do with energy. Kirsty tried hard to concentrate after that. One humiliation in a day was enough. It was only when they left the classroom for morning break (*five and a half hours, and I'll see him again*) that she noticed "coal" written in blue ballpoint pen on Toby's hand.

"Thanks for trying," she said. Toby just smiled.

Kirsty knew what to expect for the rest of the day. She couldn't sit still for a moment in the playground or even at the dinner table without Georgia or Sally saying "Wake up, Kirsty!" and waving right in front of her face so that she flinched. Even in lessons, the odd whisper of "Wake up, Kirsty!" reached her, and they would give her a little shake on the shoulder as they went past if they thought they could get away with it.

They didn't even give up when they were walking out to the bus (*just fifteen minutes to get home – then see if Mum's OK, get changed, walk up the hill – maybe an hour?*). Georgia asked her if she was off to bed now, and Sally leapt out in front of her, waving and shouting to her to wake up. It was so sudden that she had to stop with a jolt, and Sally continued dancing about and waving, stopping her from getting past. *She'd miss the bus. . .* She lifted her hand to push Sally, and stopped herself just in time.

Sally wanted to be pushed. Then she could burst into tears and limp back into school saying, "Miss, Kirsty Weaver pushed me," and Georgia would put her arm round Sally and say, "Miss, Kirsty pushed her and she wasn't even doing anything."

So she didn't push Sally. She stood still watching Sally look ridiculous, trying to block her way and waving at her. Finally, Georgia said, "Leave her, Sally, our bus goes before hers." As soon as they'd gone, Kirsty ran for the bus home, banging her school bag on to the seat beside her. She looked round for Toby but he wasn't there today, and, as she glanced out of the window, she caught sight of him in the back of a Land Rover. On any other day she might have envied him, with his kind, efficient mum picking him up and maybe taking him somewhere for a treat. *But I have my own mother and the fawn to go back to. And anyway, Toby's probably only going to the dentist.*

Sally, getting on the bus in front, leaned out to pull one more yawning face at Kirsty, who looked the other way. She tried never to be upset by anything Sally and Georgia did. Mostly, she succeeded, but it was just so annoying. Why should anyone get their fun by tormenting somebody else? Kirsty scowled, but she stopped scowling as soon as the bus began to move. It was carrying her back to the fawn.

Dad was busy in the garage when she got home, and Mum was asleep. She was dressed, though, so she must have been up. Kirsty changed and went up the hill. She knew she didn't have much chance of seeing the fawn – not if the mother had made a good job of hiding it – but the chance was worth a walk up there.

The important thing was to be patient, patient, patient. She climbed to her viewpoint and sat on the stone to watch. *The Rock Throne*, that was what she used to call it when she was little. Auntie Sarah had taught her to observe wildlife, and they had come up here together.

Everything here reminded her of Auntie Sarah, Mum's sister. She had had no children of her own, and to Kirsty she had been the perfect aunt. She and Kirsty had adored each other. Sarah was a nurse. Making things better, that was what she did. And she knew so much about animals, really useful things like how to clean oil from a bird's feathers, or heal a rabbit's cut paw. Kirsty would sit and watch her, trying to remember it all and making soothing noises to the animals. In those days Kirsty had been the Queen of the Hill with her Rock Throne, but she knew better than that now. The deer ruled the hill. Humans were only allowed to watch from a distance, so that's what she did, watching from the high stone seat.

Rabbits came out to feed. Now and again, among the trees, there would be a mottled pattern that could be the flank of a deer or sunlight through birch leaves. Then there would be a twitch that could only be a deer flicking flies from its ear. The deer were moving through the woods, stopping to graze, then raising their heads to watch for danger. One, then two, and three, made their way into the clearing, like guests arriving at a party.

The doe was there! Kirsty, recognizing the graze on her leg, clasped her hands more tightly. But unlike the others, the doe didn't stop to graze. She walked on gracefully, out of the clearing and into the bracken.

Something stirred in the bracken. Kirsty stared towards it. It could be a rabbit sheltering in there – but if she was really, amazingly lucky...

Yes! She was looking at the tiny ears of the fawn, even before its head lifted and its large eyes and little black nose appeared. The doe quickened her pace and trotted towards it as it raised its head.

Kirsty had hoped to see the mother suckle it, but she stopped, nuzzled it, and walked away. The baby scrambled to its feet as if it hadn't got the hang of standing up yet, then followed her into the quiet shade of the trees.

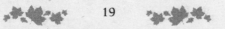

It can walk! It was only born this morning, and it can walk! Soon it had followed its mother out of sight, and Kirsty, contented, made her way back down the hill.

Back on the garage forecourt, a pair of legs stuck out from underneath a car. Dad and Mal spent a lot of time underneath cars and at first glance, Kirsty couldn't tell whose legs these were. The jeans and trainers could have belonged to either of them. A bit of muttered swearing told her it was Mal, and presently he wriggled out and sat up.

"All right, young Kirsty?" he said. "Good day at school?"

"It was OK," she said, because that's what she was expected to say. "Where's Dad?"

"Indoors. He'll be getting your tea. Better go in."

From the kitchen came the squeak-bang of the oven door. Dad must be cooking today, so she'd be doing the clearing up. They had the usual brief conversation about school and homework, and then Kirsty went to find Mum, who was now half asleep on the settee. When Kirsty came in, she opened her eyes.

"School?" she murmured.

Kirsty knew it was important for Mum to talk. She didn't want to talk about school, though, not when her head was still full of the fawn. She sat down beside Mum.

"When did I learn to walk?" she asked.

"A week after your first birthday," said Mum, so promptly that Kirsty was astonished. Mum couldn't usually answer a question without gazing ahead of her for a few seconds first. "You'd been trying to do it for weeks. You could walk around holding on to a hand or the furniture and you'd taken two little steps on your own, but you hadn't quite got it. Your dad and I were in the shed talking about what we were going to do with it, I was balancing you on my hip, and we heard a car stop outside and a door opening. I'm sure you knew it was your Auntie Sarah's car. You wriggled to get down, and when Sarah appeared at the door you toddled twelve steps all by yourself to meet her."

Kirsty handed her a tissue from the box that was always near her and folded her arms around her. Mum was already crying, probably because she'd been talking about Auntie Sarah, and Kirsty felt she might start crying herself, too. If an aunt was a long way away you could always phone her, but a dead aunt was silent for ever.

"Kirsty," said Dad later when Mum had gone back to sleep and the two of them were eating pizza in the kitchen, "I heard you talking to your mum about when you were a baby. Best not to. That kind of talk might upset her. You know. I mean, don't talk baby stuff."

Kirsty nearly asked why, but something about his look stopped her. *One more reason not to talk about the fawn. A baby thing. Anyway, it's not mine to talk about. It's the mother's. And what a lovely mum she is.*

Every morning before school, and every afternoon, Kirsty went up to see the deer, but it was only on Friday morning that she saw the mother and fawn again. It was as if the doe wanted to reward her for her patience.

As Kirsty sat on the rock and watched, the doe emerged from the trees and walked towards the bracken, raising her head. She must have made some sort of call, for the bracken rustled. Up from the forest floor came the fawn's tiny head, with bright dark eyes and a small black nose. Kirsty could feel her heart beating faster as it struggled to stand on twig-thin legs. It was as if it couldn't quite sort out which one to move next, and she bit back a giggle. But once it could stand, it trotted eagerly to its mother's side and ducked underneath her, turning its head at what seemed like an impossible angle to prod at her and find the milk. The doe turned to watch it as it suckled, as if she were proud of her baby. Nothing else in the world mattered.

You are so beautiful, thought Kirsty, and her heart seemed to grow with love for them. The mother stood patiently, twitching her ears now and again as she listened for danger, sometimes nuzzling the fawn and licking it. At last, its hunger was satisfied. It stepped back, shook its head, and gave something between a snort and a sneeze, as if its nose had been squashed against its mother for too long and needed to be shaken into its proper shape again.

The mother licked it again, and this time it straddled its legs and sent a stream of wee splashing into the grass. Kirsty pressed her lips together to keep from laughing. She didn't know why it was so funny, but it was. She was still biting her lip to keep herself quiet when the fawn obediently followed its mother to a patch of long grass where the trees cast a shade. There, it curled up like a sleepy child going to bed, and the mother stepped gracefully away into the trees, leaving it alone.

The mother's wisdom amazed Kirsty. How did animals have such powerful instincts? How did she just know what to do? But Kirsty couldn't stay and ponder this. It was time to leave the deer to themselves, as the doe had left the fawn.

All day the mother deer was at the back of Kirsty's mind, calm and watchful, with the soft-eyed fawn beside her. It didn't matter if Georgia and Sally teased her or if other people at school treated her as a bit different, and formed into little huddles that never included her, because her heart was in the green world, in the fresh, blowy wood with the animals. All day, she held the fawn and its mother like a secret treasure in her heart. As soon as she got home she'd go back, and, wonderfully, the weekend would be here. Tomorrow would be Saturday, when she could escape to the green world of the wood, and watch them as long as she wanted.

But Kirsty knew something was wrong when she was on the school bus home. The traffic wasn't usually this slow, even on a Friday. Then she saw the police car, and the policewoman controlling the traffic, so close to her own house that her toes tingled and curled with fear. She glanced round for Toby, and remembered that, again, his mother had picked him up. As the bus stopped, she saw broken glass, her father and Mal bending over something in the road, and the outstretched legs of a deer, lying still.

Chapter Three

"Don't!" she yelled. She ran past the policewoman, her hair getting in her eyes. Dad and Mal were reaching under the deer as if they were trying to heave her out of the road. "Dad, don't move it! Don't, you could hurt her!"

"There's no hurting this one, love," said the policewoman gently. "I'm afraid it's dead."

"Dead as a doormat," said Mal. Kirsty wanted to kick him.

"We've checked him over, love," said the policewoman. "No pulse, no vital signs, and we need to move him to keep the traffic flowing."

"It's a her," said Kirsty crossly.

If the power of Kirsty's will could have brought the doe back to life, she would have revived. But her dark eyes were as still as glass, seeing nothing, and her head drooped on its broken neck as Mal and Dad dragged the heavy body on to the garage forecourt. The animal who had been so graceful in life was a great ungainly weight now, making Dad and Mal strain and grow red in the face as they pushed and pulled her out of the way. Stretched out on the ground, she looked bigger than she had on the hill. . .

. . . *than she had on the hill*. . .

Than she had on the hill!

The picture was still imprinted in Kirsty's mind. Goose pimples formed on her arms.

She had observed every detail as she had huddled in the secret of those early mornings. All female deer had that shape to their heads, all fallows had those white spots. But the doe lying on the road had one ear darker than the other, and an old wound healing on her leg.

Kirsty's stomach felt queasy. She pressed a hand against it, and swallowed hard.

"It's sad, isn't it?" said the policewoman. "Are you all right?"

Kirsty nodded. "What happened?" she whispered. Her voice was failing her.

"A car hit her," answered the policewoman. "It went straight into her; she didn't stand a chance."

"Could have caused a nasty accident," remarked Mal, and didn't notice the way Kirsty glared at him.

"She wouldn't have known a thing about it, love," said Dad. "She would have died instantly. But whoever it was, they should have stopped."

"Did you see anything, sir?" the policewoman asked Dad.

"I was in the workshop," said Dad, rubbing the back of his head. "When I heard the bang I thought somebody had driven into the wall, and they were well out of sight by the time I got here." He frowned, thinking. "Tell you what, though, I could hear a noisy exhaust pipe from somewhere, but I don't suppose that's much help."

"They were almost certainly speeding," said the policewoman. "We should have speed cameras round here. I'll arrange for somebody to take the body away."

Kirsty stroked the deer's cool, coarse hair and her soft cheek. She bent over her and hugged her, as if she could comfort her. There were flakes of something blue on her coat, like old paint.

"Dad. . ." she began, then stopped. Perhaps she wouldn't tell Dad what she knew about this deer. He didn't appear to have noticed her speaking to him.

"Leave it alone, Kirsty, it's a dead thing," he said.

"It'll have ticks and fleas and all that," said Mal. "You could catch something. You don't want to touch that."

How dare you, thought Kirsty. *How dare you try to tell me what I want and what I don't want!* She stroked the deer's nose. This morning, the doe had been peacefully at home in her green wood, feeding her fawn, who was all the world to her. They hadn't wanted anything except life and peace, and now they would never see each other again. Tears came to her eyes.

"Why did she do it?" she asked, looking across the

deer's body to Dad. "They don't live down here, they live up on the hill. Why would she run down here?"

"Maybe looking for a boyfriend," said Mal. "Or food. Maybe the grass is better over there."

"It's not the mating season," said Kirsty coldly, still looking at Dad. "And they've got plenty to eat on the hill."

"Kirsty's been learning about deer, haven't you, love?" said Dad, speaking up for her as if he had to prove that she really did know what she was talking about. "She knows a lot about them."

"Sometimes a dog scares them," the policewoman told her. "People think the hills are a good place to take their dogs for a run off the leash, but it can panic the wildlife."

And deer panic easily, thought Kirsty. They weren't slow, stupid animals like cows and sheep. Deer were wild, wary and shy, alert at every crack of a twig, every footfall. A big bounding dog would terrify them – but surely the mother deer wouldn't have left her fawn? Wouldn't she stay to protect it? Or had she just run and run, deliberately leading danger away from her baby, not caring about her own safety? Kirsty rubbed her eyes.

You shouldn't have died here, on a hard grey road, lying in the open for all to see. You should be on your hill, with the grass and the stream and your beautiful baby. Did you sacrifice yourself to protect it? It'll be all right. I'll look after your baby for you. Promise.

Dad put his arm around her. "Hey," he said softly,

"I know it's sad, but these things happen. She didn't suffer." It was as if he didn't want her to talk about the deer, as if he wanted her to forget it. Perhaps he wanted to forget it himself. It wouldn't be wise to tell him what she knew. Grown-ups always thought they knew the right thing to do, just because they *were* grown up. It was no good trying to tell them they were wrong. They wouldn't listen.

"She didn't know a thing about it," said Mal.

"She must have been so scared," whispered Kirsty. She rubbed the tears from her eyes. Mal had drawn the policewoman to one side and was asking her about roadkill, and venison, and what a pity it would be to waste it. *You're talking about a baby's mother*, she thought, and something in her heart snarled at him.

"Change out of that school uniform," said Dad brusquely. "And brush down your coat – you're covered with deer hairs. And—"

"Yes, I'll look in on Mum," she said. As she ran to the house, she took off her coat and smelled the warm, animal scent of the deer's body.

The hall was cluttered with junk mail and old post that hadn't been opened. Kirsty changed into jeans and a sweater, pushed her uniform into the washing machine, and found Mum coming out of the bathroom.

"Mum, you're up!" she said, and hugged her. Mum smiled. The smile seemed to be a huge effort, but still, it was something. It wasn't "Did you have a nice day?" or "Would you like some juice?", but it was a start. Presently, Mum curled up on the settee in front of the television and Kirsty thought about the fawn, whose mother was its whole world.

She imagined it staying hidden where its mother had left it, hoping for her to come and feed it. Did it have any idea of time? Would it know how long it had waited? She didn't know, but she knew it would get hungry. It would be waiting as its mouth ached with dryness, its stomach hurt with hunger, as it longed for its mother, and she still would not come. She imagined it stumbling over the hill, calling for its mother, getting too far from the herd. At nightfall it would be wet, painfully hungry, cold and very, very afraid.

Kirsty wouldn't sleep tonight, not knowing whether the fawn was safe and fed. She knew that wild animals were best left to look after themselves. Their freedom was one of the things she liked about them. If another female in the herd fostered the baby, it might thrive. But if not, Kirsty couldn't leave it to die.

She remembered one spring Saturday, when she was only six, and Dad had taken her to Auntie Sarah's house. All the way there she had wriggled with excitement, twisting to see out of the window for the first sight of the house – but they had got there to see Auntie Sarah running across the garden, clapping her hands and shouting. As she struggled to get out of her seat belt, Kirsty had seen a ginger cat racing away and a young blackbird on the ground, struggling to fly. Dad had offered to kill it quickly and she had burst into tears, but Auntie Sarah had calmly examined the blackbird. Then she had knelt, putting her arms around Kirsty and telling her that the bird wasn't dying, it was just scratched and shocked and in need of care.

They had made a box for the blackbird and fed it from a syringe every few hours. Auntie Sarah had even got up to care for it through the night. She'd kept the box clean, and after the weekend she'd taken it to work with her, leaving it in the car. At last she had brought the blackbird to Kirsty and together they had let it go free, watched it fly, then gone out for milkshakes to celebrate. Auntie Sarah had taught her to care for living things.

Kirsty decided to go up the hill, look for the fawn, and watch it from a distance. She needed to see what was happening. Her next thought was that, while she knew a lot about fawns, she didn't have a clue about how to look after one. She'd have to find that out, and for that she needed the computer. Mum was awake, so Kirsty hugged her.

"May I go on the computer, Mum?" she asked.

"What's it for?" said Mum. It was a good sign that she cared enough to ask.

"School stuff," murmured Kirsty vaguely.

"No more than half an hour," said Mum, and Kirsty darted across the hall into the dining room where the computer sat surrounded by cluttered heaps of papers on the table. She pulled her sleeve over her hand to wipe a layer of dust from the screen and worked her way through dozens of sites about fawns and a lot of cute pictures until she found exactly what she was looking for – "How To Care For a Wild Orphan".

The first bit looked easy. If a fawn was in urgent need of feeding, it was important to give it "hydration fluid". Fortunately, Kirsty knew about that – hydration fluid was only boiled water with a little sugar and some kind of salt in it. It was what they used to give to Mum when she didn't feel like eating anything, and they still had some left. *No problem*. After that the fawn would need milk, but not the ordinary milk they had in the fridge. It would need lamb milk. What a good thing she knew where to get some!

So far, so good. She could feed him. The next thing she'd have to do would be – she looked at the computer again –

What? That!

Oh, no. I can't do that!

That is so disgusting, thought Kirsty. *I'd have to take a bit of kitchen paper and pat around its . . . its . . . its underneath bits?* She pulled a face as if she'd smelled something bad, and went on reading from the screen, which told her:

It is important to help the animal to urinate and defecate. The mother would do this by grooming the fawn. . .

Kirsty knew that "urinate" meant *wee*. She didn't understand the other word, but she made a guess and looked it up. Unfortunately, it meant exactly what she thought it did. "Defecate" meant *to eliminate bodily waste*, or, as Kirsty had thought, *poo*. According to the

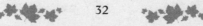

advice on the screen, a mother deer would lick and nuzzle at the fawn's bottom to persuade it to empty itself. A human looking after a fawn had to pat around its rear end with kitchen paper to get the same effect. *It's all very well if you're a deer and you're its mother*, thought Kirsty. She had sometimes imagined being a vet when she grew up, but she wasn't so sure any more.

All the same, if she had to do something really hard to save the fawn's life – if she had to sit up all night with it, give it her own food, risk being kicked by it – she'd do it. Persuading it to wee and poo was nasty, but if that was what she had to do, she'd have to get on with it. She just hoped she could get out of the way fast enough.

Anyway, it probably wouldn't come to that. The fawn would be adopted by another doe, and everything would be fine. She'd go to see what happened.

"Just going up the hill, Mum!" she called. She picked up her coat and was about to brush off the deer hairs when she thought again. Those hairs were there because she'd been wearing it when she leaned across the deer's body in the road, and it should still smell of her. If she did need to get near to the fawn, that mother-smell could make all the difference.

There was a sharp edge on the wind, a pinch of cold as she crept towards the glade where the deer grazed. They nibbled at grasses as they always did, stopping to sniff the air and twitch their large pointed ears at every sound, but there was no sign of the fawn. Soundlessly, Kirsty sat down to watch. She could stay as long as she

 33

needed to. Nobody at home would worry about where she was.

The deer gathered under the shelter of the wood. One by one, as the day grew cooler, they lay down. Kirsty watched the spot where the mother had left the fawn. Nothing moved.

She grew chilly, and had to wriggle her toes in her shoes to keep them from stiffening. She'd probably got it all wrong, and the dead deer wasn't the fawn's mother at all. Perhaps the fawn and its mother were far away, and everything was all right. But if not, if the dead deer *had* been the mother, then her baby was still somewhere on this hill, hungry and afraid.

Kirsty couldn't help rocking, very gently. Sitting still for so long was hurting, and she must have been here for an hour at least. It was time to take one slow, careful look for the fawn, so she rose as softly as she could and tiptoed between the trees, keeping her eyes down. There wasn't even a patch of flattened grass where a fawn might have lain. It might have run away. Perhaps it had gone to find its mother. *Poor baby*, she thought. *Where are you?* She had searched in all directions and was beginning a wide circle that took her in and out of the trees when she heard a strange, sad little mew.

It sounded so much like a kitten that Kirsty looked round expecting to see one, lost or trapped in a tree. But the mewing came from the fawn. Kirsty stood still.

It had wandered away from its morning hiding place, turning its large-eyed little face from side to side as it searched, its legs such slender sticks that Kirsty

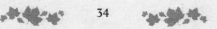

wondered how it could stand. It raised its head and mewed again. It wanted its mother, food, and warmth, so it stepped forward uncertainly, still making its sad cry, not understanding.

A doe stood under the shelter of the trees, and the fawn broke into an awkward trot as he saw her, so happy that Kirsty could imagine him smiling. She let go of the breath she'd been holding. All was well. She'd been wrong about the dead deer. This one was its mother, and Kirsty's heart felt lighter. She waited to watch the ritual of suckling and nuzzling again, as she had in the morning. The eager fawn reached the doe's side, ducked underneath her with its tiny tail flicking from side to side in excitement, and tried to suckle.

The doe turned sharply, butted it, and ran away. When it tried to follow she wheeled round, ran at it so hard that it had to skip out of her way, and darted away into the forest.

It stood alone, fragile, rejected and wide-eyed, raising its head to mew its hunger across the wood. No deer paid attention. No doe came to comfort him. Like a lost puppy, it scampered a few steps one way, then another, and Kirsty's heart hurt for it.

She had a promise to keep. Very slowly she walked towards it, making soft, soothing noises, the way she did to Mum when she found her crying and in need of a hug – *Sh, sh, it's all right, little love, you're going to be all right.* She held out her open palms towards it, watching the twitch of its ears. It stepped back a few paces, not knowing whether to trust her.

 35

And that's the trouble, thought Kirsty. *You're a wild animal, you're not supposed to trust me. But you do need to live.* Maybe it was afraid because she was bigger than it was, so she had to make herself small. Very slowly, knowing that any sudden movement would scare it, she sank down to her knees in the grass and rubbed her hands across the faded quilting of her coat, hoping to offer it the scent of its mother.

She shuffled forward, but the rustling of the grass alarmed it and it flinched, shrinking back on its hind legs. Kirsty stopped, not looking the fawn in the eyes. It mustn't feel challenged.

The fawn went on scampering from side to side again in its lost puppy way. *It's still not sure about me, so I must wait. I must stay here on my knees, holding out my deer-smelling, mother-smelling hands, waiting for it to come to me. Just wait and hope. Hope no bird rises up and alarms it. Hope no big-antlered buck chases it away. Hope nothing growls at it. Hope nothing in the grass bites it. Fawn, fawn, please come to me. Now, little one, come to me. I must be your mummy now. Little fawn, come to me. I'm your only hope. Sh. It's all right.*

The skin of Kirsty's legs prickled sharply as she knelt in the grass, and something – it might have been a fir cone – was digging painfully into her foot. Grass tickled her. But she didn't move.

The fawn took a first step, raised its head and sniffed the air. Cautiously, Kirsty stretched out her hand. It took one more step. With a shake of its head, shyly and gently it trotted to her, sniffed, and explored her coat with its muzzle. Then, with its soft nose and lips, it nuzzled her hands.

Wide-eyed, forgetting the pain in her foot and the itchy grass, Kirsty almost stopped breathing. Now, not taking her eyes from the fawn, she took a deep breath in and felt that her heart would explode with joy. The soft, warm tongue tickled her palms and made her want to flinch and giggle, but she held still and bit on the inside of her lip to keep from laughing. If she laughed, the fawn would be scared and dart away, and she'd lose it. She must be patient. With all her heart she longed to press her face against its warm neck and stroke its soft, dappled back, but that might scare it, so she only tipped her head to one side to see underneath it.

"You're a little boy," she whispered. "Good boy, good little boy." Her legs ached, but she sat still as the small, neat head pushed against her coat, sniffing at the smell of his mother. His nibbling lips teased at her fingers, then sucked them furiously.

"Come on, then," she said. "You think I'm your mum now, don't you?"

The fawn would soon realize that there was nothing except warmth to be sucked from Kirsty's fingers. So what to do next? She had brought him kindness, and couldn't take it away. From now on she had to feed him, shelter him, clean him and protect him until he didn't need it any more, and she couldn't do that by leaving him on the hill. There wasn't time to go up and down three or four times a day, and he was still small enough

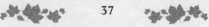

to be attacked by predators. She needed a place of safety for him nearby, somewhere quiet and empty.

The shed might do. It was roomy and near to the house, but far enough from everywhere else to keep him quiet, safe, and hidden from anyone who might want to make him into venison. She had once thought of making it a kind of secret den, and had taken an old rug in there. It could be his den now.

Steadily Kirsty got to her feet, leaving one hand in his mouth for him to suck and bending to stroke his soft neck with her other hand. The familiar smell of his mother must have clung to her coat and her hands, for he walked on beside her, keeping her hand in his mouth.

She began the slow walk back through the clearing and downhill. The fawn, bright-eyed but perfectly calm, walked alongside her, his warm tongue under her fingers.

If she'd had a free hand Kirsty would have pinched herself. She wanted to give herself a shake to make sure this was really happening. *The fawn is walking beside me, he trusts me, I can feel his heartbeat under my hand.* But any sudden movements would have alarmed him, so she walked steadily, as his mother would have, delighted by every step beside him until at last they came in sight of the shed. The fawn stopped and lifted his head, his ears and nostrils alert for danger.

First things first. There was no sign of Dad, Mal, or anyone else about. The shed door's latch was covered in cobwebs. Apart from some old plant pots and watering cans and the rug, the shed was empty. She kept her arm round the fawn as she led him into the shed.

"In you come, little one," she whispered. "You're safe here. Good fawn. You stay here. I'll be back soon." She pulled her hand from his mouth, though he tugged hard, wanting to keep her. She closed the door – the key was in the kitchen, so she'd have to make do with just shutting it for now – and ran back to the house.

Feed him. Quickly, before he gets really distressed. And if he does that mewing thing and somebody hears him and opens the door he could run on to the road, like his mum, he could run away and lose himself. Hurry. Excitement and fear made her hands tremble and she clenched them, telling herself to be strong. She knew how to be strong for Mum. She could do it for the fawn, too.

In the kitchen, where washing lay jumbled in a basket and the bin needed emptying again, Kirsty climbed on a stool to search through the medicine cupboard. *Throat pastilles, paracetamol, Mum's tablets –* there they were, the sachets of hydration salts. *Boiled water, measuring jug, stir it up – now all I have to do is – oh.*

She had no idea how to get the mixture into the fawn.

Should have thought of that. She'd imagined herself feeding it from a baby's bottle. She now realized that they didn't have such a thing in the house and there was no way of getting one (well, not unless she walked the half hour each way to town, and the chemist's shop was open, and she had enough money, however much that might be, and finally got in a blazing row with Dad wanting to know where she'd been). She'd have to use something else.

A cup. No, that was no good. The fawn wouldn't know what to do with it, and he'd only dribble it everywhere. He needed something he could suck from, and, without a useful idea in her head, she opened and shut drawers looking for inspiration. She remembered the lambs at Toby Gordon's house – there were bottles for the lambs up there, but just now she'd have to use whatever she could find.

Think. Something to suck. What do babies suck apart from their bottles? Almost everything. Thumbs. Dummies. Blankets . . . towels. . .

She whisked a clean tea towel from the drawer, dropped it into the measuring jug and stuffed as much kitchen paper as she could into her pocket. Just in time it occurred to her that she might need a torch – Dad kept one by the door, so she took that, too.

The fawn's instincts had told him to stay still, but he was mewing softly as Kirsty opened the door. With his wide eyes and spindly legs he was so beautiful, so alive, just so real, that he appealed to her as if she had never seen him before. He was such a baby! Inquisitively he took a few paces towards the door, but Kirsty shut it firmly behind her, switched on the torch and put it on the floor so that she'd have both hands free for feeding him. The torch cast only a dim circle of light, but it was a lot better than nothing. She put down the jug, took the warm soaked towel, squeezed it – not too much –

and knelt down beside the fawn as he twitched his ears and nose.

"Here now, fawn," she whispered, and reached up to pat his neck, but he retreated backwards in fear. "All right, all right. I won't hurt you. Here." She held the wet towel out to him. "It's nice."

He watched warily, his eyes on the towel, hungry and cautious at the same time. *Of course you are*, thought Kirsty. *You want your own warm mum and her milk, and you don't know what you're doing here.* She shuffled towards him, a very little at a time, rubbing her fingers on the towel and holding them out. "Here! Taste!"

Slowly, hunger and curiosity overcame him. He sniffed and licked at her fingers and sucked them as he had before, but when she tried to slip the towel against his mouth he turned his head away.

"It's nice," she coaxed. "Come on, fawn. You need to suck." *And do it soon, please*, she thought. *Sooner or later Dad will lock up the garage, and then he'll want to know where I am.*

She squeezed the towel so that a little warm fluid trickled into the fawn's mouth, and instinct told him what to do next. Ducking and turning his head as he would with his mother, he sucked urgently, looking at nothing, tugging hard at the wet towel as if nothing else existed in the world.

A thrill of excitement ran through Kirsty and glowed in her heart, a smile crept over her face, and her eyes brightened. She held the towel higher, to make the angle more natural for him. When he had sucked the towel almost dry, she pulled it away – it wasn't easy, as he fought to hold it, and it took a determined tug with both hands to get it out of his mouth. Quickly she soaked it and offered it again, giggling with delight as he pushed his nose against her hands in impatience.

"Good fawn," she told him softly. "That's better. Well done. You're all right now. You're safe." The next time she soaked the towel she had to turn her back on him, or he would have knocked the jug over. It was as if she could feel the warm drink running through his frail body, filling his stomach, making him stronger. At last the sucking became less intense, and he fed contentedly, steadily, until the towel was wrung out. He sniffed and licked at the jug when it was empty and sucked at her fingers again, but for the moment he seemed satisfied.

Now for the next bit, thought Kirsty. She swallowed hard, and straightened her shoulders. Human mothers have to change babies' nappies. If you own a pet, you have to clean up after it. This couldn't be much worse. All the same, she had an unpleasant feeling in her stomach as she pulled the wad of kitchen paper from her pocket. She'd always thought there was something very funny about rubber gloves. Now, she wished she had some.

"All right, fawn," she said. "I've never had to do this before. It's what your mother would have done, to make you let go at the other end, because if you don't you'll be ill. So stand still."

She knelt and reached under his belly, stretching

her arm out and turning her face away as she dabbed cautiously between his hind legs. "It's just a mum thing," she said, "and I have to do the mum stuff for you. Come on, little fawn, you have to. . ."

And he did, straddling his matchstick legs. Just in time, Kirsty snatched her hand away as a stream of pee splashed on to the floor.

"Well done!" she said. It was astonishing, to feel as happy and proud as this, just from persuading a deer to pee. She stroked his flank, then gently led him forward a little to get them both away from the spreading wet patch on the floor. "Now I'll have to go in before Dad comes looking for me. He mustn't know about you." She remembered all too well what Dad and Mal had said about deer being a nuisance and how tasty venison was. "No, little one, the grown-ups definitely shouldn't know about you. I'll come back soon, little fawn. I'm going to get milk for you. I'll get you everything you need."

She sat back on her heels, needing to gaze again at the delicacy of his gentle face and the velvety depth of his large brown eyes.

"I know I'm not your deer mum," she said, "but I'll do my best. I know about looking after people, because I look after my mum, so I can learn how to look after you. I know about caring. My mum's been ill since my Auntie Sarah died. I know what it's like when somebody dies, too."

The longing to wrap her arms around his smooth, soft neck and hug him was almost overwhelming, but she knew she mustn't. *He's a wild creature*, she reminded herself, *not a pet*. But she stroked his neck, because his mother would have groomed him like that.

Kneeling beside him, Kirsty felt very peaceful. Stroking his warm neck soothed her. You could tell things to an animal. With people you had to be very careful what you said. They might not listen. They got cross, and interrupted, and asked the wrong questions. Worse, they laughed at you, or thought you were making it up. Often, they didn't understand, but they thought they did. Fawn didn't understand either, but that was all right, because he didn't need to. He was simply there, like a creature of magic, and that was more than enough.

She wanted to stay but it wouldn't do for Dad to come outside looking for her, shouting her name and sending the fawn into a panic. But she moved too quickly as she picked up her coat. The fawn bolted into a corner of the shed and pressed himself against the wall as if trying to be invisible.

"Sorry," she whispered softly, and ordered herself not to do *that* again. On second thought, it would be best to leave the coat with him. It smelled of his mother and herself, mixing the two scents together, and it was something to curl up on when he was sleepy. Moving very gently, she laid it down in front of him, found the old rug she had left there, and put them together to make him a bed. Then she tiptoed backwards out of the shed, taking the jug and towel and locking the door behind her. She'd have to hide the deer feeding things in her wardrobe, where nobody would find them, and have a very good wash. *And look normal.*

Chapter Four

And Kirsty did look normal, making herself as useful as she possibly could. She helped Dad to cook tea, filled the dishwasher, cleaned the kitchen and sorted out the washing. Then she wrapped her arms round Dad and gazed lovingly up at him, hoping that she looked as wide-eyed and endearing as the fawn.

"Dad," she said, "I want to go up to the farm – Toby's farm – I mean, the Gordons'. I won't be long."

"Hart Hill?" said Dad. He didn't sound impressed. "What do you want to go there for?"

"To see the lambs," she said innocently. "Mrs Gordon invited me."

This was more or less true. The last time Kirsty had visited, Mrs Gordon had said vaguely, "Come back any time you like, any time you want to see the lambs.

Toby would love to see you. So would we." That was good enough.

"She could have spoken to me first," said Dad, but from his tone of voice, Kirsty was pretty sure he'd say yes. "Homework?"

"I've got all weekend," she said, pleading with her eyes. "It'll get done. It always does. And if I don't go now it'll be dark before I come home, and pleeeeease. . ."

She looked round purposefully at the results of her hard work – the scrubbed table, the gurgling dishwasher and the neatly spread washing on the airer. Then she looked back at him, knowing she'd won.

"Go on, then," he said. "Take care on that road, and send a text when you get there so I know you're safe. You'll not have long, mind."

She beamed and hugged him, but already she was thinking about what to put on. She'd left her coat with the fawn and she'd need something with good-sized pockets. There was an old cagoule that would have to do.

On the long walk up to Hart Hill Farm, Kirsty thought about how to keep the deer safe. The usual thing to do, if a task seemed too difficult, was to ask an adult. But as far as Kirsty could tell, adults were all too keen to blame deer for damaging trees. Anyone like Mal would shoot them, given half a chance. They might take the fawn to a vet, but vets were expensive even for cats and dogs, let alone deer. Mum and Dad didn't have that much money. And a vet might decide the fawn's life wasn't worth saving, and put him to sleep. The thought of that made Kirsty stand still in the road with her hands pressed over her face, forcing the tears back from her eyes.

No, the fawn was her responsibility, and it would be too risky to tell anyone about him. He might be killed. She'd been learning about deer for ages, long before everything at home had gone wrong. Slowly, the green world had become a much nicer place than home. It was as if she had always been preparing for the fawn without knowing it. To save this one small life, and be a mother to him when his own mother was dead, meant that she'd do whatever she had to do. She'd even steal from good people.

The big grey house with the white paintwork stood back from the road, through a wooden gate with a sign – "Hart Hill Farm" – on the gatepost. Beyond the garden, in a field that stretched away to the left, tired, shaggy old ewes grazed and bright little spring lambs played, suckled and raced. Kirsty walked down the gravelled path with the bumpy lawn on the left and a long, low, whitewashed building on the right.

Here, she slowed down. This was the lambing shed. On a chilly winter day, she had stood here to see the ewes giving birth and the tiny, creamy lambs suckling and finding their feet. Now it was quiet, dark and empty, but if she was lucky there would still be some cans of lamb milk in there. She was standing on tiptoe trying to squint through a crack in the woodwork when a loud and very bossy female voice called:

"What do you think you're doing?"

Kirsty jumped in panic. A tall dark haired girl, about thirteen or fourteen years old, was striding towards her. She wore stretchy riding trousers, a sweatshirt and long boots, and carried a helmet. When Kirsty tried to answer, all she could do was stammer.

"I . . . I . . . I came . . . came. . ." *I can't speak, and if I could, I've forgotten what to say. . . I've come to see . . . I've even forgotten his name. . .*

"I'm Kirsty," she managed at last, in a feeble whisper. "I . . . Mrs Gordon said I . . ."

"Hello, Kirsty!" called a voice. To Kirsty's relief and thankfulness, Mrs Gordon was standing in the doorway. This was Toby's mum, Toby's kind, organized, smiling mum, who had welcomed her before. "Have you come to see Toby?"

Usually Mrs Gordon was as beautifully groomed as a duchess, but today she was dressed like a shepherd. Her short glossy hair was always smooth and perfect as if she'd just come back from the hairdressers', and there was an elegant look about her even now, when she was wearing jeans and wellies and a battered old green jacket that looked as if a sheep had slept on it. Kirsty supposed it was the result of being a lawyer and a mum while living in a farmhouse and keeping sheep. *But I bet you can't draw like my mum*, thought Kirsty. She had meant to slip unnoticed into the lambing shed, help herself to some milk, and run. That wasn't going to happen now, but she wouldn't stop trying.

Mrs Gordon looked over her shoulder. "Toby!" she called. "Kirsty's here!"

Kirsty couldn't help smiling. Something about Mrs Gordon made you want to hug her, even at times like this, when you'd rather be left alone to do something you shouldn't.

The tall girl still stood in the path, swinging her helmet, looking bored.

"Tessa," said Mrs Gordon, "this is Kirsty Weaver, from the garage. She's in Toby's class, isn't that right, Kirsty? This is Tessa, she's Toby's sister." The tall girl nodded towards her and almost twitched a smile. "I'm taking Tessa for her riding lesson, but you're welcome to come and see Toby. His dad's around somewhere. Make yourself at home."

"Please, Mrs Gordon," said Kirsty – she felt a bit shy, but she had to take her chance while she could – "can I see the lambs?"

"Of course you can!" replied Mrs Gordon cheerfully. "They're all in the field!"

"None in the lambing sheds?" asked Kirsty.

"Not a single one, thank goodness!" said Mrs Gordon. "The lambing's all finished now. We've cleared the shed and scrubbed it all out, but we still have two orphan lambs indoors that we're rearing on the bottle. They're in the kitchen. Toby will show you!"

That sounded promising. As Mrs Gordon and

Tessa walked down the path, Toby appeared at the door, looking very different now he wasn't in his school uniform. At school he always looked too tidy and glossy like a new doll just taken from its box, with his neat black hair and dark eyes that looked enormous behind his glasses. In jeans and a T-shirt, with his hair a bit spiky, he looked more like anybody's brother and less like a posh kid without many friends. And, like his mother, he looked so, so pleased to see her! Nobody else gave her that happy, welcoming smile, not since Auntie Sarah had died and Mum had been ill.

"Was Mum telling you about the pet lambs?" he asked. "Do you want to see them?"

Kirsty tried not to stare at the number of doors in this house as Toby led the way through the hall. One end of the large kitchen gleamed with modern worktops, fitted cupboards and a cooker which looked as if it had dropped by magic out of a television advert. At the other end was an old-fashioned fireplace with logs in the grate and a basket of more firewood beside it. There was a rug, some comfy old chairs for curling up in, and, at one side of the fireplace, a wire pen where two curly lambs lay on their sides. When Kirsty and Toby came near they scrambled to their feet and bleated, pushing their noses against the wire.

"They always do that, telling you they're hungry even when they're not," remarked Toby. "But they probably are ready for a feed now. You can help if you like."

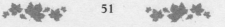

Suddenly, thought Kirsty, *I'm surrounded by hungry babies!* But feeding these two would be good practise for feeding the fawn. She followed Toby into the next room (he called it "the utility room"), where washing churned in a machine and muddy boots stood in pairs by the door. When he opened the fridge, her heart gave a little thump of excitement. Baby bottles, all filled and ready, were lined up inside the door.

Perfect! It's like a nursery! All those bottles! She watched Toby's every move, waiting for her chance. That fridge was so crammed full of bottles, they wouldn't miss one. Or two. Cans of dried formula were lined up on a shelf, and she imagined all the gallons of milk they would make. She only needed enough for one tiny fawn.

"The bottles need warming in the microwave," said Toby, pressing buttons. Kirsty watched him tap in the time and setting, because the right temperature for lambs would hopefully be right for the fawn, too. He shook a few drops of milk on to the back of his wrist, to test it.

"That's OK. It mustn't be too hot or too cold," he said, and handed her a bottle. "That's for the bigger one. They're called Rosemary and Mint. She's Mint."

"Rosemary and Mint?" repeated Kirsty. She shook milk on to her own wrist, too. It was hot, but not uncomfortably hot.

Toby opened the pen. Kirsty's lamb, Mint, pushed greedily against her arm for the bottle, sucking so hard that Kirsty needed to hold on with both hands.

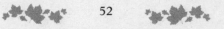

"Yeah, Rosemary and Mint," said Toby. "They're both things you eat with lamb. Dad thinks it's hilarious. Tip the bottle down a bit – if she gets it too fast, she'll be ill. The worst thing with bottle feeding is if it gets into her lungs, then she could die."

"Are these the same as baby bottles?" she asked.

"No, those ones are the wrong shape for lambs," he said. A froth of bubbles formed in the bottles as the lambs tugged at them. "These are from the farm suppliers, you can't get them in the shops. Rosemary, have you finished that already? You're a greedy little poodle, aren't you?" He pulled the bottle away from the lamb, and Kirsty almost expected her to burp.

"These two girls are ready to go out now," said Toby. "We'll put them in the garden."

The utility room door opened on a back garden where a wooden swing and a rope hung from a tree. As Toby bundled up Rosemary in his arms and carried her outside, Kirsty guessed that she was supposed to do the same with Mint, who turned out to be a lot heavier than she looked. She didn't want to be carried, either, but in spite of the kicking and struggling, Kirsty managed to heave her outside and on to the grass. Toby deftly shut the door before they could bolt back inside.

"Stupid things," said Toby, but he knelt to stroke Rosemary's head all the same. "They don't know they're supposed to be outside."

"They're not stupid," said Kirsty. Now that Rosemary and Mint had found their feet and even tried out a bit

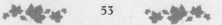

of skipping, they looked like lambs on an Easter card. "They just don't understand. It's not very kind to call them after things you eat with lamb."

Toby shrugged. "It doesn't bother them. These ones won't go for meat anyway. I expect we'll breed from them. Mum's getting all mumsy about them."

It was odd, seeing Toby like this. She rarely saw him at all in the school playground. That was probably because he was keeping away from the kids who called him "posh boy" and mimicked his accent because he said *barth* for "bath" and *dahnce* for "dance". Maybe he'd found a quiet job helping the teachers, sorting out library books or something, as a way of staying out of the way. Kids like Kirsty and Toby had to learn to cope with the continued name-calling, the footballs landing just too close to you, the whispers and giggles as you went past, and the way you'd end up alone and had to pretend not to mind.

She and Toby had a lot in common. They could be friends. But friends were people you talked to, and she mustn't tell anybody about the fawn, nobody at all. Not even Toby. Toby probably thought grown-ups always did the right thing, so he'd go running to his parents and tell them, and they'd take over, the way grown-ups did, and the fawn would be taken away.

Nobody would understand. The fawn's already lost his mum, and now I'm the only person who loves him. Nobody must come between me and Fawn. Not Toby. Not adults. Nobody. Don't even think of it.

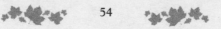

54

"We can go and see the lambs in the field, if you like," said Toby.

"Field?" said Kirsty. She was still thinking about deer.

"Field, yeah," he repeated. "I'll get some sheep nuts from the shed."

"Shall I stay here and watch these two while you do that?" Kirsty suggested, hoping she looked innocent.

As soon as Toby was out of sight, she slipped back into the utility room. A can of dried milk disappeared into one pocket, and a made-up bottle into another. She could give that to the fawn as soon as she was home, and he'd love it, and feel safe because he'd been properly fed. By the time Toby came back she was watching the lambs again and hoping the guilt didn't show in her face. Straw was sticking to Toby's sweater.

"Do you keep straw in the shed, too?" she asked.

"Course we do. Heaps of it." He led the way to the field.

Straw would be perfect for the fawn to nestle into at night. Unfortunately you couldn't stuff much of it under your sweater or into the pockets of a cagoule, but there might be a way to get hold of some. At the fence, Toby rattled the bucket of food and the sheep ran to him, the ewes shambling in their rough old fleece and the young running after them for milk.

"Greedy lot," remarked Toby. Kirsty tried to imagine the lambs, pretty and light as soap bubbles, growing up to be shaggy, pushy ewes jostling for food.

(If they get the chance to grow up, she reminded herself.) But she was getting anxious about the fawn. He'd only had hydration fluid, and he was alone in a strange place.

"We've got a pond, too," said Toby. "I can show you that, if you like. There are some ducklings just now; we might see them."

His face was eager and welcoming. He was being friendly. But the fawn needed her.

"I'd better go," she said, and felt sorry for him as the brightness left his face. "I said I'd be back before dark – I mean, well before dark. My mum worries."

"My dad can run you home," offered Toby.

"No – no, it's fine," she said, and Toby walked with her to the gate, saying little. At the gate, she looked again at the sign – "Hart Hill Farm".

"Why 'Hart'?" she asked. "And why without the 'e'?"

Toby looked a bit surprised. "It's an old word for a male deer," he said. "Hart, without the 'e'." She could see him thinking, *Didn't you know that? –* but, being Toby, he was too nice to say it, and she was grateful for that. He went on, "There are still deer in the hills. They came right down to the meadow in February, when we first came here. Everything was frozen, so they were hungry."

And my fawn is hungry, thought Kirsty. She said goodbye quickly and ran home, holding the bottle of milk under her sweater to keep it safe. She felt better knowing he'd be well fed tonight.

The fawn would need bedding, too, though. All he had to sleep on was her coat, and it wasn't very big. Kirsty hunted through the bathroom cupboard when she got home, and found some very old towels, faded and thin, which were only used when they ran out of decent ones. Nobody would miss them. She took some old newspapers, too. Better than nothing.

The fawn was mewing again when Kirsty reached the shed and shook milk on to her wrist, as Toby had done. She'd heated it up in the microwave, following the timings and settings she had watched Toby use. It felt warm on her skin, but not too hot. She'd got that right, then.

The fawn scrambled to his feet, his ears twitching, hopeful and alert, and her heart seemed to grow with love for him. Time for his first proper feed. She approached him slowly, as she knew she must.

"Here, now, fawn!" she said softly. "Lovely warm milk!"

The fawn looked at the plastic bottle as if it might explode. Nervously, keeping his eyes on it, he backed away.

"It's nice milk!" said Kirsty, but she understood. In his short life he'd only known grass, fresh air and a mother deer to suckle on. A plastic bottle with a bit of rubber on the end made no sense at all to him.

"Nice!" she said. She shook more milk on to her hand for him to lick, but the sudden movement alarmed him, making him spring away into the shelter

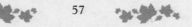

of an empty horse stall.

"It's all right!" she said in the gentlest voice she could manage – but there was nothing to do but wait, standing absolutely still, until he crept forward. *He may be shy*, thought Kirsty, *but he's inquisitive. And he knows I'm something to do with food. Come on, little fawn, you need this. If I were magic, if I were a shapeshifter, I would become a mother deer and you would be my baby. But this is all I can do, and it has to be enough.*

Delicately, the fawn stepped towards her. His wet black nose searched for the hands that had fed him before. As his soft lips nuzzled at her fingers, she slipped the bottle against the side of his mouth.

If he could have pulled a face, he would. The rubber teat must have been a strange, artificial taste, nothing like suckling from his warm, milky mother. Kirsty wanted to laugh, but she squeezed a few drops of milk into his mouth and watched as he explored the feel and the taste of it on his tongue. Then instinct and the love of milk overpowered him, and he sucked so hard that Kirsty had to take the bottle away from him now and again, afraid that he'd gorge himself and be ill. *Mustn't go down the wrong way. It can't go into his lungs or he'll die.* But as he fed, pulling intensely at the bottle, a warm joy filled her just as the warm milk filled him. Her heart lifted. When he had drained every last drop he prodded at her hands and then at the pocket where she'd put the empty bottle.

"All gone," she said. "I hope you've had enough." The website had told her what sort of milk to use, but not how much, and the bottle had been meant for a lamb. Unfortunately, it was the only bottle she had, and it would have to be scrubbed out and scalded between feeds.

"It'll have to do, I'm afraid," she said. There was kitchen paper in the other pocket. "Now excuse me while I do the other bit."

Putting food into the fawn was delightful, but there was nothing delightful about what came out at the other end. The shed would soon start to smell. The next day, she'd have to clean it out without anyone noticing, and that would be difficult. Well, nothing worth doing was easy, was it? Auntie Sarah used to say that.

Thinking of Auntie Sarah, Kirsty began to talk about her. The fawn wouldn't interrupt, and it would take her mind off the deer poo dropping on to the floor.

"I had a lovely Auntie Sarah," she told him. "She was Mum's sister. They were Sarah and Debbie, and Sarah was the older one. She was the best sort of auntie, but she got very ill and died, and that's why my mum's so sad. So now my mum's like a deer mum; she leaves me to get on by myself. All mums are different, did you know that, little fawn? I loved Auntie Sarah. I mean, I love my mum, too, but Auntie Sarah was different. She used to spoil me. Whenever we all met up she'd take me places and buy treats. . ."

She'd better stop talking about Auntie Sarah. She mustn't cry in front of the fawn, or get tears on his

beautiful soft coat. But in spite of all her efforts to behave like his real mother, she wrapped her arms about him and pressed her face against his smooth flank, feeling his warmth and the steady beat of his heart.

Reluctantly, she let him go. *I mustn't do that. It's not what a deer mother would do.* As she locked the shed, she paused.

"You'll be a hart one day," she said, "a big, strong hart, like the ones on the hill."

By the time she went to bed that night she had scrubbed out the bottle and teat, dried them, and hidden them with the tin of milk in a bag in her wardrobe. She'd put the torch in there, too. For a long time she lay awake. Since coming home from school that day, everything in her life had been transformed. She had saved a life. Everything she did now would revolve around the fawn.

He may have been tiny, but he was a huge responsibility. He could become ill, he could even die, if she made a mistake or was careless. Then there was the problem of the milk. *I'm not exactly a thief. I only did it once, and I would have paid for it if I could. And I didn't take anything for myself.*

Thinking of the milk made her remember the lambs at the farm and the fully grown sheep in the field. One day, her little fawn would be, as she had told him, a full-grown stag with antlers. Long before that, she must set him free. He had to learn to eat normal food, and find it for himself, and, most importantly, he must learn not to trust humans. She must teach him to live without her, and one day, he must forget her.

But not yet.

Chapter Five

Kirsty had her bedroom exactly the way she liked it. Nobody else ever went in there. The plain white walls would have looked better for a coat of paint, but she'd covered them with pictures, so that didn't matter much. She had pinned up all the wildlife photographs she had found in magazines and on the internet – fox cubs, otters, harvest mice, red squirrels, and, of course, all kinds of deer – as well as pictures of her family and Auntie Sarah, and various postcards Auntie Sarah had sent. Below these pictures she kept some of her presents from Auntie Sarah – *lots* of books, a wooden-handled hairbrush which she'd never used because it was too precious to use for everyday, a little bracelet, a soap shaped like a polar bear, a cuddly squirrel she called Star, and hair bobbles. There was a bug viewer, a clear crystal for catching the light which she turned round in the glow of her bedside light, although it worked better in real sun. There was a worn copy of *Jane Eyre*, which she'd tried to read but found too hard. She had kept it because she'd enjoy it one day, and it had been Auntie Sarah's own, and had her name in it.

The furniture was old and didn't match, and the pink duvet covers were the ones Kirsty had had since she'd first moved out of a cot and into a bed, but she liked them. She didn't keep everyday clothes in the wardrobe – there was no point, she'd only have to get them out again – so they were neatly heaped on chairs and the floor. Toys were pushed into a corner and the desk under the window was piled with homework, books, drawings and puzzles. The curtains at that window were one of Kirsty's great joys. She had seen them in a charity shop last year and begged Dad to buy them. In soft, glowing colours, they showed a pattern of trees and delicate leaves with thrushes eating berries, and after a year she still found them enchanting. The words *Strawberry Thief* were printed on the hem. Every night, she felt astonished and grateful to own something so beautiful, which transformed her bedroom into a magical wood, as if she were back on the hill.

Kirsty drew the curtains, stepped back just to enjoy looking at them, then kissed her fingertips and touched the picture of Auntie Sarah before getting into bed. The thought of the fawn kept her awake with excitement and anxiety. Would he be frightened? Would he be cold? Would he be hungry? After his first long, lonely night in the shed, would he even be alive? But the day had been exhausting, and she slept.

Something startled Kirsty out of sleep, and she woke suddenly from a dream about bottle-feeding the fawn. She was wide awake, and lay for a moment listening. Had he made a noise? Had he panicked and kicked out at the shed? Those spindly legs could break so easily!

In the house, doors were opening and shutting. She jumped out of bed and reached for her dressing gown. Footsteps hurried in the hall. Like a deer in the wood, Kirsty froze, barely breathing, listening for every movement. She heard the click and brush of the front door opening.

It couldn't be a burglar. A burglar wouldn't make all that noise. Looking down from the window, she saw light spilling from the hall on to the deserted yard. A man was running across the yard – oh, it was only Dad. But why was he running outside in the night? Had he heard the fawn, or was someone trying to break into the garage? Or – *no, no, no* – the shed?

She wriggled into her slippers and ran to the door. Dad was running from one side of the yard to the other, peering into the ghostly street light.

"Debbie!" he called, but not too loudly, as if he wanted to keep this as quiet as he could. "Debbie, where are you? It's all right. Come inside."

Debbie? Why was he looking for Mum? Kirsty ran back upstairs, but in the half light from the landing she saw that Mum and Dad's bed was rumpled and empty.

She glanced into the bathroom and the cluttered spare room. No sign of Mum, and Dad was still outside, calling for her.

Kirsty had no idea why Mum would have gone outside in the middle of the night, but all that mattered now was to find her. She found the torch and ran with it into the yard.

"Dad!" she called. "You'll need this!"

He snatched the torch. Above its strong bright beam, his face was terrifying.

"Where was that?" he demanded. "I've been looking for it everywhere! Get back to bed!"

"But where's Mum?" she insisted.

"Just go back to bed when you're told!" ordered Dad. Kirsty slipped back into the house, curling her hands as she watched from the door. *Don't go near the shed. Don't try the handle. Don't look for the key. Don't make a noise.*

Dad ran to the garage, and as soon as he was out of the way, Kirsty ran in the other direction. There wasn't a sound from the shed.

Where was Mum? She could be anywhere, and Kirsty's stomach tightened with fear. She ordered herself to think clearly. The mother deer had panicked. She had run into the road, and been killed. *What if...* Kirsty ran to the roadside, calling out softly.

"Mum! Where are you, Mum?"

Movement caught her eye. A figure stepped into the light from a street lamp. Kirsty approached her softly and quietly, holding out her hands, as she did with the fawn.

"It's all right, Mum," she said. "I'm here. You're safe now."

Mum's hair was wild, and she was trembling. The look in her eyes made Kirsty hurt. *If ever the fawn looks at me like that, it will be time to let him go. She looks like an animal in a trap.*

"Come back in, Mum," she said. "You look so cold. Come and get warm."

"Kirsty," said Mum, and came to meet her, seeming not to notice the hard, rough ground under her bare feet. "Did I wake you up?"

"No, I was awake," Kirsty said firmly, and linked her arm through Mum's. Mum might have been sleepwalking, but she seemed quite normal now. "Are you OK, Mum?"

"Sometimes I just have to get out," said Mum, as if it were the most ordinary thing in the world, but it sounded strange coming from someone who hardly ever left the house. Kirsty steered her mother towards the front door. Maybe it was only at night, when all was too silent and she couldn't sleep, that Mum had to get out. In Kirsty's hand, her arm felt as brittle as a dry stick.

"Debbie!" Dad was running towards them. He slowed to a walk, and his voice was suddenly softer.

"Come on, Debbie, come and get warm," he coaxed. "Come back to bed. Maybe you'll sleep now. You had me worried."

"I'm fine," said Mum, and looked surprised. "I only wanted some fresh air. What's so strange about that?" And she went quietly indoors and up to bed as if

66

nothing had happened. In the hall, Kirsty looked up at Dad.

"Go to bed," said Dad, and didn't blame her any more for being outside. "And I don't know what you've been doing with that torch, but leave it here. That's where it has to be."

"In case Mum wanders out again?" she asked, and when he didn't answer, she persisted. "Has she done it before? Dad, she has, hasn't she?"

Dad looked away as if hoping that she would have vanished by magic when he looked back. She waited. Finally, he said:

"Yes, she's done it before, but you didn't have to know about it. I didn't want you to worry. Now go to bed."

Kirsty didn't like to make him cross, but there was one question she needed to ask. It was hard to get the words out because she was so afraid of what the answer might be.

"Dad," she began, "is Mum going to get better?"

"Of course she is!" he said, but Kirsty didn't feel convinced. Dad said it as if he hoped Mum would get better, but not as if he knew it for certain. "Of course she'll be better one day. Now go to bed. It's not your problem."

Problem? thought Kirsty. *She's not a problem, she's my mum! She's ill, and I look after her as much as you do. I want her to be well.* Out loud, she only said, "I want to help, Dad."

"Just don't move that torch again," said Dad.

 67

Typical. Grown-ups. They have to get the last word.
She went upstairs, stopping to look into Mum and
Dad's room. Mum was sitting up in bed, staring ahead
of her, and Kirsty cuddled the quilt warmly round her.

"Snuggle down, Mum," she said, and kissed her.
"Sleep tight. Love you."

Then she went back to bed, knowing that she had
to be up early in the morning to feed the fawn. In
seconds, she was asleep.

The next morning, with Mum still in bed and Dad
going out to the garage with his coffee mug in his hand,
Kirsty took the bottle and the can of milk powder and,
following the instructions on the side, made up a bottle
by herself. It shouldn't have been difficult, but it was
hard to spoon the powdered milk when her hands were
shaking.

Fear was making her tremble, the fear of what she
might find in the shed. The fawn was so small and
frail, and he hadn't had a feed all night. With a knot of
anxiety in her stomach, she cleared up the spilled milk
powder and went outside.

There was no sound from the shed. Kirsty swallowed
hard as she unlocked the door, afraid of finding a cold
little body curled up on the floor with no heartbeat.

A shaft of sunlight fell through the door, and she saw
him. Lying on his side, he looked perfectly peaceful,
and as she watched, his flank rose and fell with the
soft rhythm of his breathing. *He's all right, he's all right.
His first night, and he's alive and well.* There was time

simply to kneel and gaze at him, taking in every mark on his flank, the softness of his ears, the elegance of the little head. At last, anxious to feed him his bottle, she very gently touched his back.

He woke with a start, scrambling to his feet, but to her joy, he didn't back away. He nuzzled and pushed at her, searching for milk, and before the bottle was half out of her pocket he had grabbed it, sucking as if nothing else mattered in all the world. She stood close to him, holding the bottle high, so he'd feel as if he was feeding from his mother.

She wrinkled her nose. It was getting smelly in the shed, and would soon be smellier. She'd read stories of animals getting sores from lying in damp straw, and that mustn't happen. Even the idea of the fawn feeding within the smell of his own poo was disgusting. She'd have to clean it all up, which was the yucky bit, then find some more newspapers (the easy bit), but the really, really difficult bit would be getting rid of all that dirt and mess, and doing it all without Dad seeing anything. As the fawn pulled urgently at his bottle, she imagined the problem as if she had been asked it at school.

"What would you do if you had to clean out an animal shed without anybody noticing?"

"I would wait until there was nobody about."

Dad was always busy in the garage on a Saturday morning, which was helpful, but often customers would linger outside. Kirsty sometimes saw them hanging around on the forecourt, gazing at the hills

as if they expected an army on horseback to appear against the skyline. She'd have to load all the rubbish into something before she took it out of the shed, so she wouldn't look as if she were mucking out a stable.

"Where would you dispose of the rubbish?"

"Um. . ." She couldn't put it in the wheelie bin. In a few days it would overflow and smell like a zoo. Maybe she could bury it somewhere.

"I would take it to the woods and bury it, or just cover it up with leaves. Easy."

She washed out the bottle at the kitchen sink, scrubbing the rubber teat inside out and scalding the bottle before making Mum a cup of tea. Kirsty knew lots of girls her own age who weren't allowed to use the kettle in case they spilled boiling water over themselves – *Well, try that when you have your mum to look after,* she thought as she left the mug on her mum's bedside table and took away the empty ones. She found black bin liners under the sink and was carrying them out to the shed when she heard a car engine outside.

There were always so many cars coming and going at the garage that Kirsty only noticed if the engine had an unusual sound. This one did. It chugged and grunted as if the car were trying to blow a raspberry, and curiosity made her wait to see what happened. A noise like that meant that at least one part of the car was about to drop off, starting with the exhaust pipe. Sometimes they were such wrecks they broke down without even making it on to the forecourt.

The car was dark blue and dusty. It coughed to a halt

outside the garage and two men jumped out, banging the doors so hard that Kirsty waited to see if any bits of car dropped off. They sauntered confidently towards the garage, looking it up and down as if they were going to buy it. There was nothing unusual about them – blue denim jackets and jeans, trainers, short hair, one square-jawed, with dyed blond hair showing dark at the roots, the other one mousey-haired with a jutting chin and an earring. There was something about their walk, their swagger as if they owned the place, that made Kirsty dislike them. People walked like that when they came up to you in the playground to make you look really stupid in front of everyone.

As soon as the men were in the garage talking to Dad, curiosity drew Kirsty to the car. A headlamp was broken and the bodywork around it was dented, with the blue paint flaking. Something in her memory twanged. If you were driving too fast, and you hit a deer, a fully grown female deer, what would the car look like? *Like this. Very like this.*

A noisy exhaust. That's what Dad had said.

She walked all round the car, trying to look casual and uninterested as she glanced towards the windows. A few empty drink cans lay on the back seat with two magazines, one about computers and the other with a cover picture of a girl wearing hardly anything.

Kirsty slipped out of the way before the men could notice her. She had only glimpsed them and had a quick look at the car, but something told her to keep out of their sight. *Like a deer*, she thought. She checked

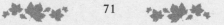

that nobody was watching before she went back to the shed.

The fawn was sitting up very prettily on her coat, which was now so dirty that Kirsty couldn't imagine ever wearing it again. She hoped the weather wouldn't turn bad. Dad didn't notice much, but he'd certainly notice if she went out on a wet day without her coat. The fawn stood up to meet her, nuzzling eagerly at her hands and pockets.

With a shovel and a bit of wood from the shed, she swept up the wet smelly newspaper, keeping her mouth shut and trying not to breathe in more than she had to. A picture of the prime minister smiling and waving and a colourful car advert disintegrated into soggy pieces as she brushed it all together. How many washes would it take to get her hands clean again? She scraped up the last fragments of the prime minister's smile with the scrappy bit of wood, to avoid touching it. The car advert disappeared in a pile of deer poo.

The fawn looked up now and again, watching as she swept, scraped, and finally got all the mess into a bin bag and carried it out, taking care to lock the shed. As soon as Kirsty was hidden by the trees and out of sight of the house she emptied it on to the grass and covered it with a few leaves and branches; then, desperately in need of a wash, she put the empty bag in the bin and went back to the house.

The blue car was still on the forecourt, lifted up by a jack as if it were sitting up and begging. There was no sign of the men who'd brought it in but Dad's legs were sticking out from underneath it, one knee a little bent. Kirsty hoped he wouldn't find much work to do on it. She remembered the flecks of paint on the mother deer's coat when she had lain dead in the road. If this was the car that had killed the fawn's mother, that shattered headlamp was like a silent witness to murder. But this murder was impossible to prove.

Kirsty ran upstairs and washed her hands. *Do it again. And again.* The dirt had gone but still she kept washing, rubbing the lather up on to her wrists, interlocking her fingers, even pressing her nails into the white bar of soap, long after the grime and smell of the shed had gone. The dirt washed off easily. The thought of the blue car and its arrogant owners, there on their garage forecourt, stayed like an ink stain. Kirsty hadn't even touched that car, but she felt it had tainted her. Finally, she raided the recycling box for fresh newspapers and took them to the shed. Seeing her, the fawn pushed the side of his face against her, searching for milk.

"You've just been fed," she said. "You can't be hungry already." He'd have to get used to the fact that she didn't always bring food, but all the same, she hated to disappoint him. In a couple of weeks she'd be able to bring him leaves from the wood, which would be a lot easier than making up bottles. He'd need water, too. She wished she could make up eight bottles at a time, as Toby did for the lambs, and heat one up whenever she needed it. She tore the paper into strips while the fawn sniffed inquisitively and got a long streamer of newsprint over his nose. Finally, she sat down beside him.

She hadn't meant to keep him company like this. He mustn't learn to trust humans, he mustn't think that it was normal for them to sit down beside you and talk to you, but it was different for her. She was being his mother. Yes, his mother might leave him alone for hours at a time, but she'd always come back. It was the only relationship a fawn would have, and it was important to him.

Anyway, Kirsty couldn't walk away from him. Just now, he was her world, and it would be easier to fly over the roof than to leave that cool, dark shed. She stretched out her hand to stroke him, and drew back again when he flinched.

"Sorry," she said. "The thing is, little fawn, I don't know how to be a deer's mum, but I'm doing my best. I'm still finding out what to do. Nobody had to tell your mum how to bring you up, she just knew, the way animals do. She did love you, you know. She tried to protect you. Mums do their best."

Her eyes blurred, so she rubbed her hand against them and went on.

"I mean, my mum does her best. She's a great mum and I love her loads, but she can't do all the mum stuff just now because she's not well. She used to laugh a lot, she used to paint, and sometimes I'd find her doing a painting of the hills and she'd flick paint at me, and she was fun! Sometimes she got low, but she always got better, and Auntie Sarah was always there when we needed her. I'll tell you about my Auntie Sarah. She and Mum weren't just sisters, they were best friends too. My mum's mum died years ago and her father lives in Spain with his new wife, so Auntie Sarah and Mum were extra special to each other.

"Auntie Sarah was a nurse. She was a really caring person, it didn't matter whether it was people or animals, she'd look after anyone. Anything. When she came to visit she used to take me to watch the deer and when I stayed at her house we'd go to an otter sanctuary, and I got to love animals, like she did. We'd watch things like *Springwatch* in the evenings, and sometimes it made her cry. She encouraged Mum to paint. But she got so ill, my Auntie Sarah. They didn't tell me at first that it was cancer, but I knew, and I knew that people get better from cancer. Auntie Sarah had to stay alive because she was the most alive person I ever knew, and she was so good, and we needed her. I thought she wouldn't be able to stop being alive. And then Mum and Dad said they'd had enough of the garage, and being here, and living by a main road. They were going to sell it all and buy a house near Auntie Sarah, so we could all look after one another, and I couldn't wait to go. But every day I came in from school and asked if anyone had bought the house, and nobody ever did."

Kirsty noticed that she was rocking as she talked. She stopped, then began talking again, but soon she was rocking again, too, without realizing it.

"None of it happened," she said. "Nobody wanted to buy this place, and all the time Auntie Sarah was

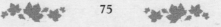

having treatment and saying she was getting better, but then she got worse, and there was nothing else the doctors could do for her. She died, and the rest of us are still here and we're not coping without her. Mum got really ill with depression after that and now it's worse, little fawn, because she spends all day in a grey house. I hate to see her like this. I want to make her better, but I can't. If only I could get her up and out, she could come up the hill, and breathe fresh air and see the deer, and I know it would help her feel better. Even if only a little bit. I don't know what else to do! I hate depression! Dad's working really hard, all the work he can get, and I do what I can, but it isn't enough."

Stop it, she ordered herself. *Stop that now. I've got enough problems without being sorry for myself.*

Kirsty took a deep breath.

"Anyway, little you, what I meant to say," she continued, "is that I know what it's like to feel lost and alone, and I know what it's like when there's nobody to look after you, and I may not be a deer, but I'll do my best. And you, little fawn, you are the only happy thing that's happened to me since Auntie Sarah died."

This time, she gave in. Sobbing wrenched Kirsty's lungs and heaved at her shoulders, while the fawn watched and listened curiously, and wondered what sort of noise this was, and what it meant. It didn't seem dangerous, whatever it was. He licked her wrist to see what she tasted of, and perhaps to remind her that he was there, like a good friend who stays beside you and doesn't make a fuss.

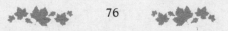

When the crying was finished, and she felt the need to wash her face, Kirsty got up. She'd need to make up another bottle of milk. She slipped out of the shed, locked it, turned and gasped.

"What are you here for?" she demanded.

Chapter Six

Toby Gordon stood in the yard. She hadn't meant to snap, but he'd taken her by surprise. She walked with him towards the house so that he wouldn't hear any noises from the shed.

"I'm not here for anything," said Toby, sounding a bit offended. "I just came down with Dad."

"You made me jump," said Kirsty. A Land Rover was parked outside the garage, with a tall man beside it talking to her father. "Is that your dad?"

"Yes, he needs a part for the Landy," said Toby, "so I came down with him." There was an awkward silence. Kirsty felt that she ought to invite Toby into the house, but the thought of it made her squirm inside. She remembered all the brightness and warmth of Toby's home, and the size of it, and didn't want him to see their faded, dusty little hall and the washing everywhere. Mum might be plodding about in her old dressing gown. Fortunately, it was a warm, dry day, so they could hang around outside.

Feeling that one of them had to say something, she asked, "How are your lambs?"

"They're fine. Yeah. Good."

Silence. She thought of the questions people kept asking her, and tried, "Looking forward to secondary school?"

He brightened up at last. "Yeah, it looks really good," he said. "I went to the open day and the science labs are great, and the school's got its own theatre. Only thing is, we have to go in on Saturday mornings, but we get long holidays so it works out OK."

Of course, thought Kirsty. Toby wasn't going to the same school as she was. She'd go to the comprehensive with everyone else, and he'd go to St Peter's in the city. They chatted a bit about schools and teachers while Kirsty kept an eye on Toby's dad, who was getting his wallet out – he was about to pay, which meant he and Toby would be going soon. That was a pity, really. She didn't ever have friends round, and she liked Toby. It was just a shame that she couldn't take him into the house. And anyway, she should really be making up the fawn's next feed. She wished again that she could do what Toby did for the lambs, making up a whole day's bottles at once and lining them up like fat white skittles in the fridge.

Kirsty was thinking about that when Toby said, "By

the way, why did you take the lamb milk?"

Hot blood rushed into her face. She tried to say she didn't know what he was talking about, but her lips wouldn't say anything and she could only stammer.

"It's no big deal, I don't mind," he said. "It's just, I always count them, and there were eight made up. I always do it like that. I'd just done them all, and then after you came, there should have been six and there were five, so you must have had one. I just thought it was a funny thing to take, that's all. What did you want it for?"

She tried to say indignantly, *Are you accusing me of stealing?* But she couldn't say anything except "What?", which sounded pathetic.

"Only, I could do with the bottle back," he said, "otherwise I can't make up a whole batch at once."

Kirsty turned on him. He was between her and the shed, and suddenly it was as if he stood between her and the fawn, too. She seized his wrist and pulled him out of sight of the garage.

"Don't speak about that," she whispered fiercely. "Don't ever, ever speak about it again. Don't even think about it." Toby tried to pull his wrist away, but she gripped it tightly with both hands.

"Hey, what's this for?" he demanded. "I don't mind about the milk. I just thought that lamb milk was a funny thing to steal, and if you—"

"Say nothing to anyone," ordered Kirsty. Her voice came out as a snarl, which she hadn't intended.

"But I only wanted. . ." began Toby. Kirsty gripped

his wrist more tightly, glaring into his eyes.

"Whatever you think I did," she said, "don't you ever mention it to anyone."

"I wasn't—"

"Promise!" she hissed.

"OK, but—"

"And if you ever, ever say anything about it," she warned, "I will. . ." – she had to think of something quickly – "I have a cousin who's in a gang and they're mean, really mean, and if you give me away I'm going to tell them where you live. Got it? And don't think that I don't mean it, because I do. I can make your life hell if I want to."

"Toby!" called Mr Gordon from the garage.

Kirsty let him go. "Remember," she said. She watched him run to the Land Rover, get in and bang the door hard. Mr Gordon waved to her. Toby didn't. He sat upright in the passenger seat, his face white and tense. Kirsty hoped she hadn't hurt his wrist badly.

A wave of hate welled up inside Kirsty, shocking and shaming her, but it wasn't against Toby. She hated herself and what she had just done. There was nothing to do but rush into the house, run up to her bedroom, throw herself on the bed, press her face into the pillow and scream. She would have slapped herself across the face, if she thought she could do it hard enough.

Why had she said those things to Toby? She didn't mean it! She'd been trying to protect the fawn, and now she felt she'd betrayed him. His kind foster mother wasn't kind at all, she was spiteful and cruel. *Bully,*

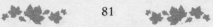

81

that was the word for what she was, and she'd never bullied anyone before. Kirsty knew what it felt like to be bullied. It was a thing she despised. In all her life she'd never tried to scare or hurt anyone. She helped to look after Mum. She was kind to small children and animals.

Bully. Just thinking the word make her eyes fill up. It was a horrible, ugly word. A horrible, ugly thing. What would Auntie Sarah have thought of her? She curled up as tightly as she could, as if she could hide from a disappointed Auntie Sarah, or even from herself. But perhaps the worst of it was that, just for a second or two, as she had gripped Toby's arm and snarled in his face, she had meant it.

She had to be willing to protect the fawn at any price. His deer mother would have done anything to keep him safe, but she was an animal without a sense of right and wrong. *I know right from wrong*, thought Kirsty, *and I turned on Toby. Toby, who is one of the nicest people I know, Toby, whose parents welcomed me into their beautiful home. They won't like me now.*

She rubbed her eyes and looked away from the "Auntie Sarah" corner in her room because it made her feel even more guilty. She relived the scene. Toby hadn't been angry, or threatening. He hadn't even called her a thief. He'd asked her very politely why she'd wanted lamb milk. He didn't seem to have mentioned it to his parents – he'd even been trying to explain something as she had grabbed his wrist and terrified him.

Kirsty sat up, hugging her knees. She had to

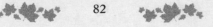

82

apologize, and try to make things right with Toby. To do that, she needed to explain why she'd stolen the milk, and that meant telling him the truth.

Kirsty swallowed down her tears, and tried to think sensibly. However much she wanted to keep the fawn secret, she could do with an ally. What if she were ill and couldn't get to the shed and do his feeds? Somebody else would have to look after him, and why couldn't that be Toby? He was kind and friendly, and knew about animals. Clever, too. Surely he would understand why she was doing this, and that the fawn needed her?

Kirsty sighed. She knew now that the fawn wasn't the only one in need of help. She needed to trust somebody with her secret. She wanted that somebody to be Toby, but first she would need to prove how sorry she was.

Prove it. She could give him a present, as a peace offering. Dad could be a bit vague about pocket money, but he always left some cash in a kitchen drawer so she could help herself to dinner money, and the money for any household shopping she needed to do. She thought about buying Toby some chocolate, but that seemed too easy. He'd think she was trying to buy him for the price of a couple of Mars Bars or something, and be insulted. She needed to give him something that really mattered.

The most important things to her were presents from Auntie Sarah, but they were mostly girl things. She picked up each one at a time. Was a crystal too

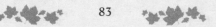

much like a girl thing? Probably. The bug viewer – he was sure to have one of those already. Hairbrush. Hair bobbles. The books. The copy of *Jane Eyre* was very special because that had been Auntie Sarah's own, but he wasn't likely to want *Jane Eyre*, was he? Kirsty sifted through the rest of them. *Alice Through the Looking-Glass* – no, not right either. *Skellig.* She'd enjoyed that one, with the creature in the garage that might be an angel. She had read it when Auntie Sarah was ill, and thought that if she'd had an angel in the garage she'd ask it politely to get off its angelic bum and make Auntie Sarah better, because they couldn't do without her. Well, she didn't have an angel in the garage and now she didn't have an Auntie Sarah, either. She had a sick mother and a baby fawn to look after, and not much time for reading. She put the copy of *Skellig* in her bag, ready for school on Monday morning.

Kirsty picked up the hairbrush again, feeling the smoothness of the wooden handle, and stroked it against her hand. It was too special to use for herself, but the fawn needed to be groomed now and again. It wouldn't be a waste to use Auntie Sarah's gift for him. It would be like bringing the fawn and Auntie Sarah together. She left it on her bed, ready to take with her when she went to feed him again. *But first, wash up, see if Mum wants anything. Make up bottle – too hot – leave bottle to cool. Put washing away. Eat. Cut up some fruit for Mum, stand over her to make sure she eats it. Feed the fawn, find a dish to put water in for him, because he should always have fresh water.*

When Kirsty went to the shed, the fawn ran mewing to meet her, and she hid the bottle behind her back. She didn't like to keep it from him when he wanted it so much and she longed to feed him, but he had to learn not to make a noise. If he didn't get the bottle when he mewed, and did get it when he stopped, he'd get the message about keeping quiet.

"Sh!" she said, still holding the bottle behind her back. The fawn stopped mewing, which impressed her very much until she saw that he'd only stopped because he had worked out where the food was and was trotting round her to reach it. Before she could transfer it from one hand to the other he was pushing and fighting for the rubber teat, so that she found herself turning round on the spot while the fawn got the bottle into his mouth and she had to go on turning until she was facing back the right way. *This is not behaving like a mother deer*, she told herself, *and a mother deer wouldn't laugh out loud because the fawn won*. She remembered just in time to hold the bottle high, and pull it away now and again so he didn't gulp it down too quickly and choke himself. She stood close against his side, so he would feel as if his mother's warm flank was against him.

Now that Kirsty was becoming used to it, even toileting the fawn was good. It was a few more precious minutes spent in this magical world with him.

"Look at this," she said. "I've got something new for you."

She took out the hairbrush, ran its softness against her hand, and then stroked it gently along his back. It

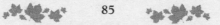

wasn't altogether a successful attempt at grooming, as the fawn seemed to think that a hairbrush might taste nice and kept turning round in an attempt to get it into his mouth, but she supposed he'd get used to it.

Kirsty looked at him carefully. She'd never get tired of watching him.

"What do you think?" she said. "My friend Toby's got two lambs called Rosemary and Mint, and I have to call you something. It seems all wrong because names are what you give to pets, and you're not a pet. You're just Fawn. And there's nothing better that I could call you, because it's exactly what you are. Fawn."

She wished she could have stayed longer and watched him fall asleep, but there was homework to be done, and the bottle must be washed out before the next feed. It was time to lead him to his rumpled bed, shake out and smooth the rug and the coat (she didn't like to think too much about that ruined coat), and watch as he tucked in his front legs, knelt, and snuggled down into his nest.

"You are beautiful," she whispered, and planted the gentlest kiss on the top of his head. "I'll be back for your night feed." Then she crept silently away.

Kirsty went to bed that night too tired for a shower and woke with tangled hair, forcing herself to get out of bed and make up a bottle. More homework. Over the weekend her hair grew straggly, and she scrubbed and scrubbed to get the dirt out of her nails. She scrubbed the bottle and the teat, too, when nobody was there to see. But whenever she walked into that shed, whether to feed Fawn or to clean, she felt she had stepped into the green world of the hill and the door had shut behind her. Her fawn, her baby, who wanted nothing but milk and warmth, looked forward to her coming. Tiredness could not follow her here. Neither could homework, nor worrying about Mum.

At home, she took care over everything she said and did. Mum and Dad mustn't notice that she was sneaking to the shed. They must never see the bottle or find the supply of milk. She must dust herself down or change after she'd been to feed Fawn. But it would be good to share the secret with somebody. She found she was looking forward to Monday, and a chance to make it up with Toby. At least, she hoped so.

Monday morning came, a cool morning in spite of the time of year, and Kirsty hugged herself as she stood at the bus stop. It wasn't a day to be out without a coat. Toby stood with his back to her and ignored her, and she couldn't blame him. She was about to start on her apology when the bus arrived. Toby got on without even bothering to glare at her and sat down beside somebody else to make it quite clear that he didn't want to talk to her. The copy of *Skellig* in her school bag was like a live thing, wriggling to be out, but Toby made a pretty good job of avoiding her all day and she had to wait until afternoon break before she had the chance to talk to him.

He was late coming out of the classroom, and she

waited for him at the end of the corridor. When he saw her he turned to go the other way, and when she ran after him he quickened his pace.

"Toby!" she called. "Wait! *Please!*"

He clearly hadn't expected her to say *please*. He stopped, but didn't turn round.

"I wanted to say sorry," she said.

He turned to face her, still not speaking.

"I'm really, really sorry," she said. "About what I said. And what I did. I was horrible, and I'm not like that. I've never done anything like that before. Honest." When he still didn't speak, she went on. "I don't hurt people. I don't do threatening and all that."

"You did this time," he said.

"I know, and I said I'm sorry. It was because . . . it's complicated. I only did it because I was scared."

Toby looked away and she remembered that she hadn't been the only scared one. She took a deep breath.

"I was scared because I had to. . ."

There was a brisk clip-clip of heels along the corridor behind them. Mrs Baines, their teacher, appeared with a coffee mug in her hand.

"Kirsty! Toby! Outside at once!" she ordered.

"Miss, can I get my bag out of the classroom?" asked Kirsty.

"You don't need it. Out!" said Mrs Baines.

No chance to get the book, then. They went out to the noisy, busy playground, and to Kirsty's relief Toby didn't run away from her as soon as they were outside.

She sat down against a wall and he sat beside her. He didn't speak, but he was ready to hear what was coming next, which, she felt, was more than she deserved.

"Thanks," she began. "I haven't got a cousin with a gang, and I'm not scary. Honestly—"

Toby interrupted. "Yeah, I might believe you if you hadn't nearly broken my arm. I only wanted to know what you wanted lamb milk for, that's all; it's a funny thing to take. If you don't want to tell me, you don't have to. You just didn't have to get so stroppy about it."

"I've never ever stolen anything before. . ." she began.

"Whatever," said Toby. His patience must be running out. She took another deep breath.

"Can you keep a secret?" she asked.

Toby turned his head to look at her at last. "Are you trying to look after a lamb?" he asked.

She hadn't expected this, and it made her laugh. Then she saw that it was a perfectly sensible question. You steal lamb milk, you want to give it to a lamb. It's obvious.

"Because, if you are, it's not one of ours, we haven't lost any, but it must belong to someone. What's so funny?"

"No, it's not – I haven't got a lamb." A football hit the wall just above their heads so that they ducked, and somebody laughed. They both knew it had been done on purpose, and ignored it.

"I need to know that you can keep a secret," she said. "You have to promise."

"I can't promise if I don't know what it is," said Toby.

This was very reasonable, and also very annoying. He couldn't make a promise to keep a secret if he didn't know what sort of a secret it was. She couldn't tell him without a promise. They were stuck.

"Look," Kirsty sighed, "if you promise and then I tell you what it is – and then you find it's something bad and you think you shouldn't have promised – I won't hold you to it, all right?"

Slowly, in the most irritating way possible, Toby shrugged. "Maybe," he said.

Kirsty couldn't help admiring the way he stood by what he thought.

"Can you come to my house after school?" she asked.

"Maybe," he said again.

"Will you or won't you?" she insisted.

"It'll depend on homework," he said, "and whether I'm allowed to."

That would have to do. She tried hard to think of something to say, and asked, "How are Mint and Rosemary?"

"Oh, they're great," said Toby, grinning and relaxing at once. "They still need bottles, but they're turning out strong. They'll be fine." They both ducked to avoid a well-aimed football. "Do you suppose they're aiming at you, or me?"

"Both of us," said Kirsty. Two misfits together must look like a pretty good target. Toby went on talking about the sheep – at least, Kirsty thought he did, but she wasn't really listening – until the bell rang.

Kirsty had hoped to give Toby the book on the bus home, but he was sitting next to another boy and she didn't want to talk in front of anyone else. At home she found Mum dressed and sitting at the kitchen table, but looking wretchedly ill. She was turning the pages of a catalogue – *junk mail*, thought Kirsty – but didn't seem interested in it.

"Cup of tea, Mum?" said Kirsty brightly, putting the kettle on. She hugged Mum, and told her about her day – *Mrs Baines says we have to do a project about pollution. Toby and I are going to work on it together. Do you know anything about pollution, Mum? Do you think I should do one about petrol fumes?* She put her hands over the catalogue.

"You should read something funny, Mum," she said. "Or something cute. Shall I put on a DVD?"

Having settled Mum in the sitting room with a DVD, Kirsty had the kitchen to herself. She made up a bottle, changed into the clothes that smelled of deer, and went out to the shed, opening the door very gently, not wanting to startle Fawn.

Asleep, Fawn lay with his delicate hooves neatly tucked in, his eyes closed and his long eyelashes lying dark against his cheek. Kirsty knelt beside him, watching every breath, adoring him.

She hated to disturb him, but she couldn't wait for ever. She stood up, shook the bottle, and watched as he blinked himself awake. Then he stretched, a long, smooth stretch like a cat, flexing his slender legs and arching his neck. He scrambled to his feet, gave himself a shake and turned his head to the sound of the milk swishing in the bottle. He pushed his face against her sweater as he searched for the food.

"You greedy little gobbler, it's the milk you want, not me," she said, but she was deeply, wonderfully happy as he pulled at the bottle. "Aren't you beautiful?"

When Kirsty had fed and cleaned him she left, slowly and reluctantly, reminding herself that his water bowl needed refilling. She'd go and see what Dad was doing, too, and let him know she was here. But as she locked the shed and looked across at the garage, she felt suddenly cold, and a bit sick, and a shiver ran down her spine.

That blue car was there. The memory of the two men sprang to mind again, the blond one with the square face and the mouse-haired – no, *rat-haired* – one. They had parked the car very close to the garage, facing towards her. The blond one was sitting in the driving seat, his eyes turned towards the wing mirror. Kirsty stood back. She knew it wasn't helpful to interrupt when Dad was busy with a customer, and with these customers, she didn't want to go near anyway.

She was still watching from a distance, looking at the man in the car and wondering what he'd seen in the mirror that was so interesting, when she saw him reach forward to turn the key in the ignition – then, with a rush and a bang of the door, the rat-haired man leapt from the shop and jumped into the passenger seat. As Dad ran out, the car was already moving. Dad threw himself at the bonnet, but with a roaring engine the car accelerated, swung past Kirsty so close that she stumbled as she heard the driver's laughter, and swerved towards the main road. Dad stopped running after them, out of breath.

"Kirsty, love, are you all right?" he asked, taking her by the shoulders.

"Yes, I'm fine," she said a bit crossly, because she'd had a shock. "Idiots!"

"Never mind them, I thought you'd been knocked over," he said – and though she was shaken and angry, she saw the way Dad looked at her, with fear and anxiety in his eyes. It was as if she was all that mattered, and she wished he'd look at her that way more often – but he was holding on to her too tightly, and his fingers were digging into her.

"Ouch," she said.

"Sorry, love," said Dad, and let go.

"What happened?" she asked. "Were they stealing from the shop?"

"Drove off without paying," he said. "I'd just reached for the PIN machine when he was off, and of course his mate was looking out for him, ready to go. They think they're smart, but I've got their number. I can get the police on to them. Nothing to worry about. In you go, and don't tell. . ."

"Don't worry," she reassured him. "I won't tell Mum." As if she would! What did Dad take her for? They were always very careful about what they told Mum. School, outings, parties, the local wildlife, anything like that was OK to talk about. If Kirsty had fallen off her bike,

93

or been in trouble for forgetting her PE kit, or Dad was struggling to work out the VAT and fill in the tax form, Mum wasn't to know about any of that. She mustn't be upset. Kirsty had had a lot of practice at not telling Mum things, and was very good at it.

Dad was no longer gazing at her. He was looking past her at somebody else.

"Hello!" he said. "I've seen you here before, haven't I?"

Kirsty turned. To her delight, Toby stood a metre away, his face pink as if he'd been running.

"Hi, Toby!" she said. "Dad, it's Toby from Hart Hill Farm – Toby Gordon. He's come because we've got school stuff to do."

This wasn't quite true, but it was the right thing to tell Dad, who nodded briefly at Toby and went back to the garage. Still not wanting to take Toby indoors, Kirsty sat down on the doorstep.

"What's up, then?" he asked.

Starting from the Monday morning, Kirsty told him about Fawn's birth, the mother feeding him, and her death on the road.

"I heard there was a deer killed," he said. "Did you see it?"

"Her, not it," Kirsty said. "She was dead on the road, and I knew which one she was. I recognized her; it was Fawn's mother. Now, come with me and don't make any noise."

With a glance over her shoulder to make sure nobody was about, she walked to the shed and unlocked it.

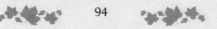

Fawn lay on his rug, his head up, one foreleg curled underneath him and the other stretched out. When he saw her he stood, shook himself and trotted to meet her.

"You've been fed," she said. "I suppose you think I've brought you more. Sorry."

She turned to Toby. His eyes were wide with astonishment, and his mouth hung open.

"Wow!" he whispered.

At the sound of a strange voice, Fawn sprang sideways. He bolted into the darkness of the horse stalls and Kirsty sighed with relief.

"Good Fawn," she said.

Chapter Seven

"He's amazing!" whispered Toby behind her. "He's beautiful!" Then, in a normal voice, he said, "What's he doing in here?"

Kirsty ignored him, walking slowly to Fawn, holding out her hands, calming him, giving him time to prod and hunt and work out that there was no more milk. She stroked his flank, patted his rump, made soothing noises, then stepped away backwards, still watching him as he watched her. *Take care not to step in anything*, she reminded herself. She'd need to clean the floor again tonight, and just the thought of it made her tired. It had been a long day.

"We'll go up the hill and I'll tell you all about him," she said, speaking to Toby but still looking at Fawn. "Don't try to touch him."

Fawn turned his head suddenly and licked at his flank, and she watched him a little longer. It was wonderful, the way he simply knew how to do that, just as he knew how to stretch, and suck, and – thank goodness – to hide, if he had to. She ushered Toby out, locked the shed and led the way up the hill.

All the joy of Fawn was new again, now that she could share it with Toby. She wouldn't be alone any longer, and for the first time since the doe had been found on the road, she relaxed. Fawn's reaction to Toby was encouraging, too.

"He was alone on the hill. He would have died if I'd left him," she said. "He's getting used to me but he ran away from you, and that's good. It means that he hasn't learned to trust all humans, just me, and with any luck he thinks I'm some sort of a deer, cos I mixed up his mother's scent with mine. If we go this way we might see the herd."

As they walked up the rough path, where brambles and long grasses reached out spiky, sticky fingers, Kirsty told Toby all there was to tell about Fawn. She told him all she'd learned about how to take care of Fawn, and why she was afraid to tell anyone.

"All the grown-ups I know seem to think of deer as a nuisance," she said, "or a dinner. Either way, they want to shoot them."

"My mum and dad aren't like that," argued Toby. "And the vet wouldn't be."

"The vet would probably just say he couldn't be saved, and put him to sleep," she said.

97

"I'm sure she wouldn't," insisted Toby. "Our vet wouldn't."

"And vets are expensive," said Kirsty, though she knew that money wasn't a problem in Toby's family. "And at a vet's he'd meet lots of people and get tame, and he mustn't do that. He mustn't get used to people if he's going to go back to the wild. He mustn't trust humans."

"Yes, I see that," said Toby thoughtfully, and she could see that he understood what she was trying to do. He knew that she didn't mean to keep Fawn for ever.

"That's why I was glad when he ran away from you," she explained. "I'm the only human he knows, and I've done all the mother deer stuff for him. It's only until he's old enough to go free."

"When will that be?"

Kirsty wasn't sure. Even after all she'd read, she could only guess.

"I reckon a few months, depending on how he's doing," she said vaguely. "When he's bigger and stronger, and can look after himself. I think I'll know when the time's right." *I hope I will.*

"I still think my mum and dad would help," insisted Toby as they plodded uphill. "They don't like the deer eating their young trees, but they wouldn't kill him for it. And they could pay for a vet."

Kirsty stood still. "Please," she said, knowing all that she could do was ask him to keep quiet about this. She couldn't make him. He pulled up a few grass stalks, rubbed them in his hands and tried unsuccessfully to make a whistle.

Finally, Toby said, "Will you promise that if he gets ill, or hurt, or anything, we get an adult to help? Because then we'd need to pay a vet."

That was reasonable. "Done," she said, and they slapped hands to seal the bargain.

"Look!" said Toby.

They were on the edge of the clearing. Behind the trees, half-hidden among the tree trunks and branches, a stag had lowered his head to graze. Powerful antlers moved against the greenness.

Kirsty watched. One day that would be Fawn, strong and free. It was hard to imagine while he was such a baby, but this was what he would become – or he would so long as she didn't fail him – and by the time he looked like that, he would have forgotten all about her. That was how it had to be.

"I can get you more milk for him," Toby said. "And bottles."

"Thanks," she said. "I need that."

"And you need to clean up his mess."

"I already do that."

"Yeah, but there's some special disinfectant for mopping the floor," he said. "I can get you some of that, we've got loads."

They turned and began to walk back downhill. "I could do with some hay," she said. "But. . ." – she couldn't quite look him in the eye – "I couldn't hide that in my cagoule."

Toby laughed and stuck his hands in his pockets. "Yeah, he should have some hay, or straw, or both," he

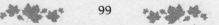

said. "There must be some way of getting it here. And I could help with his cleaning out."

"I suppose so," muttered Kirsty. She didn't want Fawn to become used to humans, but part of her reason for telling Toby about him was to give Fawn another carer, if ever she couldn't be there.

"Maybe it would be OK if I wore your coat," he suggested. "So I'd smell like you?"

"He's already got my coat," she said. "It's not really a coat any more, it's more of a bed."

Toby laughed. "I'll have to go soon," he said. "Can you come to my house after school tomorrow? We'll raid the lamb supplies. I'll ask if you can stay for dinner; nobody's going to mind."

Kirsty was puzzled for a moment before she remembered that Toby came from the sort of home where the evening meal was *dinner* or *supper*, not *tea*. "I'll have to come here first to feed him," she said.

"And sometimes I can come here," said Toby hopefully. "And if there's nobody in the kitchen I can help with scrubbing bottles and stuff. I'm good at that."

Kirsty couldn't help glancing at the house. Sooner or later, she'd have to let him through the door.

"It's a bit difficult," she said. "My mum's not well."

"Oh, what's the matter?" asked Toby.

She nearly snapped *None of your business*, but then remembered that she didn't want to quarrel with him again. "Just not well," she said, and was glad that he didn't ask any more.

"The parents might think it's funny if we're always at

100

each other's houses," she said, thinking out loud. "Or at least, mine will. We could tell them we're doing a school project. A project about wildlife, so they won't think it's funny if we're always trying to find out about deer."

"We're supposed to be doing pollution," said Toby, but very soon they had worked out that they could always do the effects of pollution on wildlife, and a deer being killed on the road was a sort of pollution, so looking after an orphaned fawn was about the effects of pollution on wildlife and they'd be telling the truth. No problem there, then.

A car glided into the yard, and Kirsty recognized it. It was the one Toby's parents drove when they weren't using the Land Rover.

"Mum's come for me," said Toby, and didn't look pleased about it: "I told her I'd walk back by myself." The car stopped near the shed – *too near the shed,* thought Kirsty. *Don't bang the door.* She found she was thinking those words towards Mrs Gordon as if she could push them into her head by sheer force of will. *Don't make a noise.*

"Toby!" Mrs Gordon called brightly, leaving the door open. "I had to nip over to the supermarket, so I thought I'd pick you up on the way back. Hop in! Hello, Kirsty!"

"Can you wait just a minute, Toby?" asked Kirsty. She ran back to the house and came back with the copy of *Skellig.*

"It's a present to say sorry," she said.

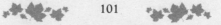

"Oh." Toby looked surprised, and not sure what to say as he looked down at the book in her hands. "There's no need for that."

"Yes, there is," she said. "Take it. Please."

"Thanks," he said, but something in the way he looked and spoke gave him away. He'd already read it. *Of course he has*, thought Kirsty. *He's probably got his own copy. I bet his bedroom's full of books. He has to understand what it means.*

"It's a special one," she said, "because I wanted you to know I was really sorry and I meant it. It was from my Auntie Sarah."

"But if it's from your auntie. . ." began Toby.

"No, that's why I want you to have it," Kirsty said, and pushed it into his hands. He must have seen that he'd hurt her feelings if he refused, so he took it with a smile. It was a smile as if he'd been given a twenty-pound note, not just a book.

"Thanks!" he said happily, and turned to his mum. "Mum, can Kirsty come to our house tomorrow?"

"That depends on her parents," said Mrs Gordon. "Do you want to ask them while I wait?"

Kirsty explained that Dad was still working and Mum was – er – Mum was having a rest, but of course Mrs Gordon insisted that she should ask. She slipped indoors and found Mum just awake enough to say "Yes, of course, sweetie." She probably didn't know what she'd been asked, but it was good enough. Mrs Gordon seemed to be satisfied, and Toby turned, beaming widely, to wave to her as they left. He looked as if all his birthdays had come at once, as Auntie Sarah used to say.

Was he so thrilled about Fawn, or just happy to have a friend? Kirsty wondered if he'd had a proper friend since the Gordons came to live here. Perhaps not.

The familiar warm, slightly sour shed smell met Kirsty as she took Fawn his next bottle. She saw him standing in a shaft of the fading sunlight as it fell through the skylight.

"You are so beautiful!" she whispered as she smoothed his back. His eyes glazed over in concentration as he tugged at the bottle. Already, she was sure, he was growing bigger and stronger in her care. She could bring him solid food, too, but he should have sunlight, and room to run around. On the hill he would have been learning how to sniff at the air, to recognize danger, changes in the weather, and all the sounds and smells of the outdoors. The only natural smell here was his own pongy one, which would get worse as the weather grew hotter. Kirsty found she was looking forward to Toby bringing the disinfectant for the floor. "I'm looking forward to scrubbing a shed floor now," she said. "That's what you've done to me, Fawn."

By the time she got back indoors she'd been splashed with deer wee – *oops, should have got out of the way faster* – so before tea she put all her clothes in the wash and herself in the shower. Since Fawn had arrived she'd completely taken over the washing so that Dad wouldn't notice any strange smells or stains. *But he wouldn't*, she thought, as she stood under the spray of water and rubbed shampoo through her hair. Mum or Auntie Sarah would have wanted to know why her clothes smelled funny, but not Dad.

"Where have you been?" Dad asked crossly when she came downstairs. *Isn't it obvious?* thought Kirsty, as her wet hair clung to her neck, but she didn't want to say anything to make him even grumpier.

"In the shower," she said meekly.

"I've been calling you for the last ten minutes," he grumbled.

After tea he asked if she had homework, and, of course, she had. There was maths, which she hated, and spellings to learn, and after that there would be Fawn to feed again, and the washing would have finished its cycle and be ready to hang up . . . for the first time since Auntie Sarah died, Kirsty felt a surge of anger against Mum. *What do you have to be depressed for? I miss Auntie Sarah, too, but I have to get on with things. Why can't you help me? Why can't you at least help me with my spelling, like any other mum?*

Immediately, Kirsty hated herself for thinking that. She hadn't invited that flash of temper. It had just slipped into her tired head from somewhere. Mum couldn't help being ill. *I just can't go on coping with everything*, she thought. So she curled up on the settee beside Mum to practise her spellings, whispering the words and the letters out loud because she thought that might help her to stay awake. Her eyes wanted so much to shut. . .

Mum jumped to her feet so suddenly that Kirsty jumped, too. Mum stood in the middle of the room, turning slowly and looking from one side to the other like a searchlight.

"I heard him!" insisted Mum. "He was crying!"

"Who was?" asked Kirsty innocently. Mum ran to the front door and threw it open.

"Can't you hear him?" she demanded wildly.

Kirsty listened hard, and at last heard a very faint cry. From the shed, Fawn was bleating like a lost lamb, calling for her to feed him. How had Mum heard it from inside the house?

"There's nothing there, Mum," she said, and took Mum by the arm. "Maybe you need to go to bed."

"No!" exclaimed Mum crossly, and suddenly turned on Kirsty. "I don't need you telling me what to do!"

"All right!" said Kirsty to keep her quiet, but she closed the door.

"It sounded like a baby!" said Mum. "You must have heard it!"

"I can't hear anything," said Kirsty firmly. "There's no baby. It's cold here." It wasn't, but she needed to get Mum inside. "Please, Mum, come and get warm." She was steering Mum back into the sitting room when Dad appeared and put his arm round Mum's shoulders and sat her down.

"It's all right, Kirsty, love," he said. "This has happened before." Then, to Mum, he said very gently, "He's not there, love. You know that. You know about the baby. He doesn't cry."

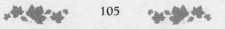

Suddenly, to Kirsty, it was as if they were speaking a foreign language. What about a baby? Mum put her hands over her face and wept, quietly.

"It's all right, love," soothed Dad, and turned to Kirsty. "You'd better go, love. I'll explain later."

Kirsty did as he suggested, and, while they wanted her out of the way, she took Fawn his next bottle. For the minute, the shed seemed to make much more sense than the house. Fawn bleated as she came in.

"Sh!" she said, putting a finger to her lips, but Fawn didn't understand "sh", and ran to her, still bleating. As she had done before, she tried to hide the bottle behind her back – *I know it's hard, but you have to learn to be quiet, so I won't give it to you when you bleat* – but again he seemed to think it was a game, and ran round her to find it. She held it out of his way, but he stretched up for it and she hadn't the heart to taunt him. Soon, he was sucking hard on the bottle while she stroked him.

"I think I love you more than I love my mum," she said, and felt shocked at herself for saying so. But then, saying it out loud made her realize that it wasn't true.

"No, I don't mean that," she said. "I love my mum all the way through, I always have. It's just that you're easier to love." *Mum isn't a sweet little thing with big brown eyes and a strokable coat, but she's my mum, and she'll be there when you're not. She's there for me in her own way.*

"There was a cat hanging around the shed, Mum," she lied when she went indoors and found Dad rocking

Mum in his arms. "That must be what you heard. It's gone now."

"Are you sure that's all it was?" asked Mum. Her face was tear-stained and her eyes red-rimmed, and she looked far older than she really was.

"Yes, just a cat," Kirsty reassured her. She didn't like lying, but it seemed like the only thing to do.

"Did you see it?" persisted Mum.

"Yes!" said Kirsty. "It was a gingery one." She really wished Mum would stop asking. The lie was getting bigger.

"Was it all right?" asked Mum. "Was it hurt?"

"It was fine," said Kirsty. "It just saw me and did that crouchy thing that they do, then spat at me and ran off."

I'll start believing in the cat myself if she doesn't stop, thought Kirsty. But Mum finally seemed content.

"A cat," she murmured, and the anxiety left her face. She sat up. "Of course it was. Now, Kirsty, let's see about your homework."

If Mum had suggested a trip to Calcutta, Kirsty could not have been more surprised. A few minutes ago she'd been in tears because she thought she heard a baby crying. She must be making a great effort now to put that behind her and take an interest in Kirsty. What followed was all three of them having a happy, chattery time that made even learning spellings entertaining. Kirsty couldn't see why she should have to know the spelling of "hyacinth", but she saw that, as they talked, Mum had picked up a pencil and was idly drawing a

bluebell shape on the back of an envelope, with "wild hyacinth" written in elegant script underneath it. Kirsty smiled. Mum drawing, especially drawing flowers, was always a good thing. When they were both yawning, Mum told Kirsty to go to bed, but Kirsty slipped into the kitchen first to have a word with Dad.

"What was all that about babies crying?" she asked. "Why was Mum going on about a baby?"

Dad sat down on a kitchen stool. He patted another one, for her to sit down.

"When you were little," he began, "too little to know what was going on, your mum was having another baby. He was born too soon."

"Premature," said Kirsty, to point out that she was old enough to know the right word.

"Premature, yes, very premature," he said. "And born dead. Your mum was very low for a long time, and sometimes she'd wake up in the night and say there was a baby crying somewhere. She'd be so convinced about this baby crying, she'd go hunting all over the house looking for him. It's as if, because he never cried, she feels as if he has to. This isn't the first time she's heard a cat or something and thought she heard the baby crying. She hasn't done it for a long while, though, and you were never there before when it happened."

"That's so sad. Poor Mum," said Kirsty. Then she thought of Dad, who would have liked a little boy to bring up. "Poor you." She imagined what her little brother would have looked like, and what it would be like to be a sister.

"Did he have a name?" she asked. Dad smiled and put his elbows on the table, and she knew he was enjoying this chance to talk about the baby. "Your mum liked Joseph and I wanted Ben. Then we thought about letting you choose, but you were such a little dot, you would have called him after Paddington or something like that. But when he was born, he was Joseph."

Tears were rising in his eyes. Kirsty gave him a quick hug and went to bed, not saying anything. That was the best way. She left the light on for a while, her head turned towards her green world curtains, wondering what it would be like to have a brother.

Joseph. My little brother Joseph. This is my brother Joseph. Our Joseph. Come on, little Joseph, hold Kirsty's hand. Where's Joseph?

And she'd never even known that he existed.

She fell asleep thinking of him. That night, she dreamed of a toddler Joseph waddling about the forecourt, always with his back to her. She never saw his face.

Chapter Eight

If Dad hadn't been clattering noisily about in the kitchen next morning, Kirsty would have slept in. She dragged herself slowly from the warmth of her bed, splashed cold water on her face to wake herself up properly and waited until Dad was out of the way to make up Fawn's bottle and take it to the shed.

"I just learned something new, Fawn," she said. "I had a little brother. At least – I don't know if it counts if he was never alive, but it counts to me, because now I'm thinking about what he would have been like. My brother. I had a brother. Kirsty and Joseph. That sounds right, but it feels funny. I wish they'd told me before. I shouldn't talk to you so much or you'll end up thinking you're human, but I need to tell you about this."

A bubbly noise from the bottle, and Fawn loosening

his hold, told her that the milk was already finished. Fawn nosed at her for more.

"You're not getting enough, are you?" she said. "I'll have to start making two bottles."

She took the Auntie Sarah brush and groomed him. The white patches on his flank seemed clearer now. She wished she had a mobile phone or a camera, or could draw as well as Mum, but all she could do was observe Fawn, every detail of him, the shade of his coat, the exact shape of each white patch, his tiptoe hooves and the wide, twitching ears. But nothing, no picture, not even a photograph, could ever capture the wide brown eyes under their dark lashes. With a huge effort, Kirsty turned her back and left him, to get ready for school.

The good thing about bad days is that they come to an end, that was what Auntie Sarah used to say. Kirsty already knew that some days at school were far too long. On this day, for Kirsty, it was such a thoroughly bad, miserable school day that it couldn't end soon enough.

Firstly, by the time she'd fed Fawn that morning she'd been in such a hurry to get to the school bus that she'd tripped over the post on the doormat and bruised her arm. Then when she got to school she found that she'd forgotten her kit for PE, and had to wear whatever Mrs Baines could find in the Lost and Leftover Box. At least it was all clean, but she ended up in a top too short for her, shorts too big and plimsolls that kept slipping off. It's hard enough being an odd one out when nobody notices you, but it can be even harder when they do.

The hall smelled of old school sweaters, school dinners and polish. Mats, beanbags and climbing bars were set out in rows. With the rest of the class neatly dressed in their navy and white kit, Kirsty curled her toes in the badly fitting shoes. She could feel the gazes of Georgia and Sally watching for her to do something really funny and embarrassing. She couldn't help tugging at the short T-shirt, but when she caught sight of Georgia and Sally also tugging at their T-shirts and then giggling behind their hands, she'd decided not to do it any more, even if the T-shirt did ride up (which it did). The baggy shorts, which she'd tied as tightly as she could around her waist, made her feel so ridiculous that she couldn't even run fast. When a shoe flew off and everyone laughed, Kirsty laughed, too, so that she'd appear to be taking it well, but inside herself, she writhed.

"Love the baggy shorts, Kirsty!" said Georgia as they were changing afterwards.

"Baggyshorts!" whispered Sally as they stood in the dinner queue behind her.

I have Fawn, thought Kirsty as she stared ahead of her and pretended not to notice. *In my secret world I have Fawn, and you know nothing about him, and I don't care what you think about me. You have stupid faces and squeaky laughs, and I have Fawn.*

The thought of Fawn held her later, as Sally jogged

her elbow when she was working. Since Fawn had arrived, bedtimes had been later and getting up had been earlier, so that she couldn't help yawning, however hard she tried. She did her best to hide it. Georgia and Sally would be watching. She bent her head down over her desk, hoping that they couldn't see.

"Good thing those two don't go on our bus," remarked Toby as they left school.

"Baggies!" said Sally and Georgia as they walked past, patting their mouths with their hands. Kirsty shrugged. She was going home to warm, living Fawn, and what were they going home to? Computer games? But she couldn't relax, even when she was sitting beside Toby on the bus. It was only when she stood between the shed and the house that she could shake off the day and take a few deep breaths of fresh air.

"I brought another bottle," said Toby. He shuffled through his school bag and brought out a sealed plastic bag with a bottle inside. It looked like evidence from a crime scene.

"Thanks. I think he needs two of these at each feed now," she told him, unwrapping the bottle. "He's getting hungry between feeds. He was mewing in the night last night, and my mum. . ."

She hesitated. She did want to tell Toby about Mum and little Joseph. She just hadn't got used to the idea herself yet.

"Your mum what?" asked Toby.

"She thought she'd heard something. A cat or something," she said. "She got worked up about it."

They were still hovering outside the house, and Kirsty wondered what sort of mess it would be inside. She had to go in to make up the bottles and it would be unfriendly to leave Toby outside in the yard, but she still wasn't keen to let him in, either. She could give him the key to the shed, and he could go in there ahead of her, but that would confuse Fawn. She had no choice.

"You'd better come in," she said, bending her head because she felt that her face was red. "Sorry about the mess."

At least the rubbish had been taken out. Nothing had been hoovered, dusted or tidied, though, and a large cobweb hung from the ceiling. It looked like something left too long on a washing line, and forgotten about. *I bet they don't have cobwebs at Hart Hill.* But to her great relief, Toby didn't notice the shabbiness and messiness of the house, or if he did, he was too polite to mention it. He couldn't help looking at that cobweb, though.

"Stay there," she said, and, hearing Mum's voice, peeped into the sitting room. She was watching TV, and looked tearful. Kirsty hugged her.

"I'll make you a cup of tea, Mum," she said. "Then I'm going to Toby's later, OK?"

In the kitchen, she made tea and – quickly and expertly by now – mixed two bottles of milk for Fawn. Toby stood watching and irritating her by asking about things. The morning's post lay in an untidy heap on the table.

"What's that?" he asked.

Kirsty looked down and frowned. "It's Dad's VAT return; I'll have to remind him to do that. He always leaves it till the last minute."

"And this one?"

"It's about MOT tests; it should be in the garage. Don't separate the pages, whatever you do."

"There's one from the police."

Kirsty looked at that one. It was something to do with tracing the owner of a car, and probably meant that Dad was trying to find the men who'd driven away without paying. The blond one and the rat-haired one. She put it back exactly where it had been, so Dad wouldn't know she'd been looking.

"And that round thing's a bit of an engine," she said, as Toby reached out to touch a metal cylinder that lay on a chair. "He shouldn't bring things like that in here. Mum would be livid if she . . . if she knew." She had nearly said "if she cared", but stopped herself just in time. "While you're here, you can put the mugs in the dishwasher and the milk back in the fridge."

"Who's that?" he asked, looking at a photo on the fridge door.

"That's my Auntie Sarah. She died."

"Oh." There was a pause, then, "The Auntie Sarah who gave you *Skellig*?"

"Yeah." She shook milk on to her wrist.

"Don't you want it back, then?"

"No. I told you. I want you to have it. The milk's still a bit hot. I'll take the bottles upstairs to cool." Seeing his puzzlement, she added, "Well, I can't leave them here, can I, where somebody could find them! Then, while we're waiting, we can go and see the deer on the hill if you like."

"Can't we go and see. . ."

"No," she said firmly, though she wanted to see Fawn too. "It's nearly feeding time. It's not good for him to have us going in and out all the time."

"Yeah, I understand that," said Toby. All the same, Kirsty could tell he was disappointed. She left the bottles upstairs, took Mum her tea, and led the way back outside, quickly. She was saying something about how long it would take for the milk to cool when she realized that Toby wasn't listening.

He was looking across at the garage, and at a large agricultural lorry parked outside. It was loaded with bales of hay.

"Come on," he said. Kirsty followed him, wondering what he was planning.

"We could ask the driver for some of that hay," he suggested.

"He wouldn't give us any," said Kirsty. "And even if he did, he'd ask what we wanted it for."

Toby stuck his hands in his pockets and appeared to consider this.

"OK, what if it just fell off?" he said.

Dad had seen them and came to meet them, asking the usual questions about school and homework, and as usual Kirsty said everything was fine. He asked how Mum was, and Kirsty said that she was "a bit, you know", which was a way of saying that Mum wasn't too good. Dad looked as if he would have gone straight to the house, but the phone in his pocket rang. He walked away to answer it, but Kirsty could hear some of what he said.

"Andy Weaver – Weaver's Garage – oh, thanks for getting back to me. Yeah, wherever they are, I had a letter from them this morning. Not the sort of letter you'd like. . ." Then he walked away, lowering his voice.

What letter? wondered Kirsty. She'd seen the morning post. She and Toby had just been looking through it, and there was nothing to worry about. She remembered pushing it out of the way as she picked herself up off the doormat in the morning. Four letters.

Four, but there were only three on the kitchen table, and the parcel from the spare parts people – that was what she'd tripped over. She remembered another letter lying on the mat, a small white envelope with the address written untidily by hand. That must have been a letter that Dad didn't want her, or Mum, to see. *Wherever they are . . .* wherever *who* are?

She looked round for Toby, but he had wandered over to the lorry and she supposed he must be behind it now, as she couldn't see him at all. As she looked for him, she was surprised at first to see that the driver had left the tailgate of the lorry down. If he drove away like that, the hay really could fall off.

A bale began to move, jerkily, as if it had learned to shuffle and was trying to escape. Kirsty walked round quickly to the other side and saw that the tailgate was

 117

down because Toby had opened it, and was tugging hard at a loose bale, first one side, then the other.

"You can't do that!" she whispered urgently, and glanced round to see where the driver was. Fortunately he was still in the office, waiting for Dad. "Stop it! That belongs to someone!"

"It's no worse than stealing milk," Toby whispered back as he heaved at the bale. "You could give me a hand; don't just stand there."

"If he gets in and reverses, you'll be knocked down!" she whispered urgently. "And if you leave the tailgate open, it'll all fall out!"

"Yes, but I'm not stupid enough to leave it, am I?" argued Toby hoarsely, still tugging at the bale. "And he won't come back yet because he's waiting to talk to your dad, and your dad's talking on the phone, and I could do with a hand here."

He gave one last pull, and the hay bale toppled to the ground with wisps of hay drifting around it. Without a second thought, Kirsty darted round to the other side of the lorry and pushed the tailgate shut. One on each side, they hooked it deftly into place. Kirsty glanced over her shoulder.

"Dad's finished on the phone!" she whispered. "He's in the office!" He appeared to be looking for something on the shelves, and she prayed that it would take him a while to find it. Toby was taking off his coat.

"Get it behind the tyres!" he ordered, so together they shoved the heavy bale behind the heap of tyres, squeezing their eyes shut as dust from the hay blew in their faces. At the sound of the garage door opening they gave one last shove, but one end of the bale was still sticking out. Toby threw his coat over it and sat on it. Kirsty tried to sit down beside him, but there wasn't room and she fell off.

"You all right, love?" asked the driver as he walked back to the wagon.

At that point, something strange happened to Kirsty. She knew the right thing to do would be to smile, nod, and tell him that, yes, thanks, she was fine. But she couldn't say anything. She wasn't usually a giggler, and she fought to keep her mouth under control, but there wasn't a thing she could do about it. Giggling rose up and completely overwhelmed her, and all she could do was to sit on the ground and shake with helpless laughter. The driver looked at her as if he wasn't sure if she was laughing or in pain.

"She's fine," said Toby. "She's always like this."

The driver grinned as he got into the cab and drove away. Kirsty struggled to breathe and wiped tears from her eyes. Toby glared at her.

"What was that for?" he demanded.

"I couldn't help it," gasped Kirsty, and folded over again.

"You nearly got us caught," he said. Looking up, she saw the scowl on his face.

"Sorry." The giggling stopped as suddenly as it had started, as if someone had flicked a switch. "I don't know why I did that. I didn't mean to."

Toby still didn't look pleased, but he wasn't fierce

any more.

"We have to take this seriously," he said.

"Seriously!" she repeated. She was ready to tell him that she was the one who rescued Fawn in the first place and she was taking it perfectly seriously, but she started to laugh again instead. She couldn't help it.

"We need to get this into the shed," he pointed out.

"Sooner or later," said Kirsty, "Dad will put up the sign saying 'back in ten minutes'. Then he'll go home to check on Mum, and while he's there he'll go to the loo because there isn't one at the garage. If he's going to be longer than that he'll put up the half hour sign, but I think he'll just give himself ten minutes. When he does that, we can move the hay into the shed."

They were debating how long it would take before Dad needed the loo, and whether Kirsty should take him a cup of coffee to hurry him up, when he left the garage, hung up the sign and strode purposefully to the house. Like two furniture removers, Kirsty and Toby took the bale and, with a lot of effort, pushed and pulled it to the shed door.

"Stay there a minute," she said, while she slipped quietly back to the house to fetch the bottles from under her bed. Toby held them while she opened the door.

"Stay by the door, absolutely still, and don't make a sound," she said. "Don't draw his attention, don't try to speak to him. I'll lead him to the other end of the shed, so he's out of the way."

Fawn had heard the opening of the door, so that

Kirsty had to shut it smartly as he ran to meet her. It wasn't much of a run, more of a skip and a jump, as if he was still trying out what his legs would do.

"This way," she said, and walked to the far end of the shed with Fawn following her, nudging and pushing with his nose, searching for milk. He hadn't noticed Toby bringing in the hay at all. He only wanted his bottle, and nudged at her with his head until he got it. She pictured him in the wild, filling his stomach with milk, feeling his mother's warm underbelly against his face, so she pressed his head gently to her side and stroked his coat. Today she didn't want to say anything, only to feed the heart-beating, beautifully alive creature under her hand. School bullies, homework and washing had no place here, in the green world. It felt as if a protecting love enfolded Fawn and herself.

"Good Fawn," she said at last, when there was nothing in the bottles but milky bubbles. And that was when she realized that she hadn't brought any kitchen paper to tickle him at the other end and make him pee, and she really didn't like the idea of doing *that* with just her hands.

"Toby," she said, "can you bring me a handful of hay? Quickly, we don't want him to run away."

She held on to Fawn tightly, her arms round his neck, while Toby brought her the hay she had asked for. Then he stood still, gazing at Fawn as if he had just stepped out of a fairy tale, while Kirsty said "Stand back" just in time to prevent him getting his shoes wet.

Fawn shook himself, then jumped. Kirsty, who

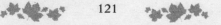

hadn't expected this, jumped too. Just in time, Toby darted back as Fawn kicked his heels out, bucked, jumped again, and bolted to the other end of the shed.

"Is the door shut?" called Kirsty.

"Yes!" said Toby. Within inches of the door, Fawn swerved, tore back towards them, turned, and dashed across the stable again, skipping, bobbing, jumping on the spot, and kicking up his heels. Kirsty and Toby pressed their backs against the wall, to give him room.

"What's he doing?" whispered Toby.

"I think he's just playing!" Kirsty whispered back as Fawn kicked up clouds of dust from the floor and bounded into the air for the sheer fun of it. He turned and ran straight at her.

Her first instinct was to dodge out of the way – but, no. *Think like a mother deer. She wouldn't move out of the way for him.* Kirsty stood her ground as he sprang towards her. He checked himself, whirled round and ran away again, his tail flying up behind him. Energy filled the air around him, it filled the stable, it filled Kirsty, who found she was laughing because laughing was the only thing to do.

All this time, Toby stood still, his eyes fixed on Fawn as if he were watching a unicorn or a dragon, something magical and mythical, not a young deer from the hill. Even when Fawn ran to within inches of him and veered round again in a whirr, Toby remained on the spot, motionless.

Fawn didn't tire, or slow down. He just suddenly stopped. Then he twisted to rub his cheek against his foreleg, trotted to his water dish, drank, and lay down elegantly on the coat, folding his forelegs beneath him. It was as if he had given them permission to go.

"Hay," said Toby.

"Hey, what?" said Kirsty. She was still thinking about Fawn dancing.

"*That* hay," said Toby. "There's no point in leaving it here all baled up."

"Oh, *that* hay," said Kirsty, and they pulled handfuls of hay from the bale to spread around the floor, then walked out into the sunshine. Neither of them spoke. They were still treasuring Fawn's outburst of energy in their hearts. They sat down with their backs against the shed door and Tony gave a long breath out, as if he hadn't dared to breathe in the shed.

"Little *star!*" whispered Kirsty, then turned sharply to Toby and said, "Fawn, not you." She wiped hay dust from her hands.

Toby found his voice at last. "Wow!" he said.

"All that running about," said Kirsty. "I've never seen him do that before. It's exactly what he should be doing. In the wild, they do that. I must be doing something right."

"I reckon you're doing a lot right," said Toby. "He's amazing." Then he pointed out that his mum would be wondering where they were, and when Kirsty had said goodbye to Mum and Dad, they walked up to Hart Hill Farm. They talked about wildlife and pollution and what to put in their project, but neither of them were interested. Fawn was in their hearts and minds, not to

 123

be left behind.

The first thing Kirsty noticed, when they stood in the hall of Toby's house, was Tessa, walking up the wide staircase while talking on her mobile phone. Tessa had changed out of her school uniform and put on jeans and a t-shirt, but even so she looked as crisp and clean as a brand new book. As Tessa paused at the top of the stairs, Kirsty suddenly became aware of what she herself must look like.

Her hair hadn't been brushed since the morning or trimmed for months. Her old cagoule was bundled over her arm. There was a stain on her T-shirt, her jeans were dirty from the shed floor and she didn't have to look at her hands to know that they were grubby and her nails needed scrubbing. She had left her shoes in the porch, and could feel the hole in the toe of her left sock. She only hoped she didn't smell of deer pee. A tortoiseshell cat stalked into the room and sniffed inquisitively around her.

"Mac likes you," said Tessa in a commanding voice, as if she were giving an order. "He's very interested in you."

So I do smell, thought Kirsty, and leaned down so that she could stroke the cat and hide her burning face at the same time. *Toby probably noticed, too. I should get out now. I should go home. I'm all wrong here except when I'm feeding sheep.*

But she didn't go. She knew she had to stand her ground in the sunny hall, and try not to stare at the bright, fresh paintwork, the wide staircase and the number of doors – all around her, and above her, and on the landing, too. How many people were supposed to live in a house this size?

The door beside her opened. Mrs Gordon appeared, today in jeans and a rather pretty cream T-shirt and ballerina shoes. She was holding a phone to her ear.

"Shall we make it Thursday, then?" she was saying. "Thursday at eleven – twelve? That's fine. Looking forward to meeting you." She switched off the phone and beamed down at Toby and Kirsty, asking them brightly about what sort of a day they'd had, and homework, and Kirsty, how are all your family?

"They're OK, thanks," said Kirsty, and felt cross with herself, firstly for lying and secondly for sounding stupid. "It's very kind of you to let me come, thank you."

Mrs Gordon laughed. "Nonsense, we love to see Toby's friends," she said, though Kirsty suspected that "Toby's friend" might be more to the point. "You don't have any brothers and sisters, do you?"

Any brothers or sisters? For the first time in her life, Kirsty had to think about this question.

"No, I'm the only one," she said, because she knew that little Joseph wasn't supposed to count, even though he *did* count, very much, to her. There was an awkward silence. Then Toby broke it by suggesting that they should go to see the lambs, and Mrs Gordon said that they could let Rosemary and Mint out into the field. Toby and Kirsty went out to the sheep-smelling utility room – a much nicer smell was coming from the kitchen – and shooed the lambs outside.

"How many pockets have you got?" asked Toby. "I can let you have another bottle, and you can make one up here, ready to give him when you get home."

"You've already given me two," she said. "It'll spoil your system."

"Doesn't matter," he said. "And you can have some more milk powder, and you'll need the disinfectant for the floor."

"We've got some at home," she said. She couldn't see how she was going to hide one of those large bottles of disinfectant in her pockets, and besides, she wasn't happy about taking so much stuff from Toby's family. All right, Toby was one of the family and was offering it to her, but it didn't feel completely right. When they heard Mrs Gordon coming they both darted guiltily away from the store cupboards and took bottles from the fridge to warm up for Rosemary and Mint.

"Do you like lasagne, Kirsty?" asked Mrs Gordon.

"Yes, very much." At least she could tell the truth about that. "I love lasagne."

When they sat down to eat, Kirsty was very glad she'd said that. The lasagne on her plate wasn't at all like the kind they got for school dinners, or the ones they occasionally had at home, from the freezer. This was a rich, strong taste, with creamy cheese sauce and warm flavours that she recognized, though she didn't know what they were. There was something familiar about it. Perhaps Mum used to make it like this when she was well, or Auntie Sarah did. She looked up at Mrs

126

Gordon in awe, and saw that Mrs Gordon was watching her with a quiet smile. Kirsty suddenly felt awkward, and managed to say, "This is lovely, Mrs Gordon."

"You're most welcome," said Mrs Gordon. "David says I should use more garlic and pepper. That's the way he does it when it's his turn to cook."

So Toby's parents both cooked like this! Did he know how lucky he was? She ate slowly to make it last.

"Anyone for seconds?" asked Mrs Gordon when they had all finished. "Kirsty?"

"No, thank you," said Kirsty politely, who would have loved more, but didn't want to appear greedy. The delicious meal and Mrs Gordon's kindness made her feel even more guilty about the milk, so when they'd finished she decided to be as helpful as possible, carrying plates through to the kitchen, rinsing them and putting them into the dishwasher. Then, because she was used to doing everything at home, she brought in the washing from the line in the garden and folded it neatly.

"My word!" said Mrs Gordon. "I wish my children were as well trained as you!" Tessa gave her mother a withering look, which Kirsty pretended not to see. "You two can have the computer now, if you want it for your homework." Then just as Kirsty was leaving the kitchen, she said, "Kirsty, how's your mum?"

"She's all right, thanks," Kirsty replied. It was what she usually said.

"Toby said she's not well," she said.

"Oh," said Kirsty awkwardly. "Um – well, no, she's not. But she's sort of all right, thanks." Then she escaped to the computer, leaving Mrs Gordon wondering about this shy child who was so expert at cleaning and tidying, but who always looked dragged through a hedge and whose mother clearly had problems.

Kirsty and Toby settled down to work on their project, looking at everything to do with pollution and wildlife. Presently Tessa came in and started talking about how her friend's pony nearly choked on a crisp packet.

"That's pollution," she said firmly. "And traffic's pollution; even the noise is a pollution because it scares ponies. So do loud bangs, fireworks and gunshots, they all scare horses, and so do badly behaved dogs, and that's just the noise. Ragwort's poisonous to horses but you mustn't use pesticides on it because they're dangerous, too, and horses can eat the bits out of helium balloons when they come down, and those new Chinese lanterns, they have a—"

"Tess-mess," interrupted Toby, "shut up. We're doing stuff about wildlife, not your pongy ponies."

"Der!" said Tess. "If it works for ponies, it'll work for wildlife, yes?" And she marched out as if she were about to declare war on ragwort and Chinese lanterns.

"But she's right," said Kirsty. "Why do you call her Tess-mess?"

Toby grinned. "Because it really, really annoys her," he said.

Toby's father gave Kirsty a lift home. She sat upright and very still in the passenger seat, afraid that the milk would slosh noisily in the bottle. She was concentrating so hard on this that she hardly noticed the blue car until it was swinging out in front of them with a roar of smoky exhaust fumes, too fast, and – Kirsty shut her eyes – much too close. She lurched forward in her seat.

Chapter Nine

Mr Gordon braked sharply. Kirsty rocked back into her seat and opened her eyes.

"What does he think he's doing?" snapped Mr Gordon, and added more gently, "Kirsty, are you all right?"

"Yes," she said, a bit breathlessly. As they stopped outside the house, Dad ran out.

"Did you see them?" he demanded. "Which way did they go?"

Mal came running from the workshop shouting something to Dad, but he stopped at once when he saw Kirsty and Mr Gordon. Before anyone else could speak, Dad was rattling out orders to Kirsty.

"Kirsty, go and see if your mum's OK," he told her. "Don't tell her anything's wrong. If she asks, it's just some idiot with a noisy engine, right? Mal, get on the phone."

But the first thing Kirsty did was to hang up the cagoule carefully, not wanting to spill the precious milk. Mum was coming out of the kitchen.

"Did you have a nice time at Toby's?" she asked.

Wow! Mum remembered where she had been, and cared about whether she'd enjoyed it! Kirsty started to tell her about the lambs, then stopped when she realized that Mum wasn't listening any more.

"That engine noise has stopped!" said Mum.

"Dad must have fixed it," said Kirsty. "I think he went out to see about mending it. Do you want anything?"

"There was breaking glass," murmured Mum, as if she were talking to herself.

"It's OK, Dad's sorted it all," said Kirsty quickly, and changed the subject. "You know the sheep at Toby's house? They have two little pet lambs called Rosemary and Mint. They get bottle fed. They can go out and eat grass now, but they still like bottles, and then their tails wag. . ." Mum still looked worried, so Kirsty tried harder. "Look, they do it like this." She crouched, craned her neck up and wiggled her bottom in the best impression she could do of a bottle-feeding lamb. "And then if it's empty, they run after you. . ."

It was working. Mum was laughing! Kirsty caught her and clung on, dancing her round the kitchen. "This is the lamb dance," she said. "You have to stick out your bum, like this. . ." Making Mum laugh was an even greater achievement than rearing Fawn. It

 131

was a timid laugh, as if Mum was out of practice, but a laugh all the same.

Dad marched in. He looked puzzled and pleasantly surprised to find them doing a silly dance and laughing. He rummaged in the cupboard under the sink for a dustpan and brush, and marched out again.

"What do you need that for?" asked Mum.

"Some idiot threw a bottle out of a car," he called back. "It landed in the middle of the forecourt. I'll sweep up the glass before somebody drives over it."

Mum frowned. "There was a lot of noise," she said. "I wondered what was happening." The brief joy seemed to leave her, like a thick cloud blotting out the sun. But it had been there, that flash of sunlight. Sunshine was still there, behind the cloud.

Later, when Dad had come back in and he and Mum were out of the way, Kirsty took two bottles and slipped out to the shed. It bothered her that she hadn't said a proper goodbye to Toby's father and she hoped he didn't think badly of her because of that, but as soon as Fawn pranced towards her nothing else mattered. He searched for his bottle, and sucked with milk trickling down the sides of his mouth.

"Too fast," said Kirsty, lowering the bottle so he wouldn't take it too quickly. When it was empty, he nuzzled for more and grabbed at the second bottle, too. Before he had finished it, he lost interest.

"Sensible Fawn," she said. "You know how much to have. Now stand still to be brushed." In a long sweep she stroked the brush along his back. Fawn's ears

132

twitched, and a moult of fine brown hairs followed the line of the brush.

"This isn't just any old hairbrush," she said. "This is Auntie Sarah's hairbrush, and anything from Auntie Sarah is as good as magic." She stroked him, feeling the slenderness of the bones under the skin. "You feel as if you're made of sticks. One day you'll be a great big ginormous stag with antlers, and you'll go bellowing over the hill in the autumn."

Kirsty was tired, deeply and hopelessly tired, by the time she'd finished, and the floor still needed cleaning. It would be easy to leave it till the morning, but she had more time now than she'd have then. She left the shed and came back with disinfectant and a bucket of hot soapy water and began to scrub the floor, leaving an unpleasant air of deer poo and disinfectant. *And the weather's getting warmer*, she thought. *Come midsummer, this shed will stink to high heaven if I don't keep it clean.* Fawn tugged at the hay, tasted it and lay down.

Scrubbing the floor was hard, heavy work at the end of a long day, and Kirsty felt ready for a bath long before she'd finished. She pulled some more hay from the bale for him, sniffing the fresh, clean smell of it. It would be a lot nicer to sleep on than her coat, which by now looked like something she'd found on a rubbish heap.

"How do you get things so dirty?" she said. "You don't go anywhere. What do you do to get grubby? I'm talking to you too much, but I can't help it."

She had bundled up the bottles, buckets and all the rest of the things that she'd needed and was about to leave when Fawn decided to have a run. She couldn't miss this. She stood back against a wall and watched him, marvelling at the way he could whisk himself round and never lose pace. From the main road, a siren screeched. Fawn froze. Then he leapt into the shadow of a horse stall.

Kirsty followed him. He stood so absolutely still, so deep in the shadow that if she hadn't seen where he went, she might not have found him. Pressed into the dark space, he seemed to be making himself as small as possible.

Her first thought was to comfort him, as you would a small child. She wanted to stroke him, reassure him and tell him everything was all right, it's only a fire engine or something, it won't harm you. But he mustn't learn that. He mustn't lose the instincts that could save his life in the wild. She must turn her back and walk away from him, as his mother would. Putting her feet down as noiselessly as she could, she crept away, locking the door behind her.

There was a pleasant evening light and a breeze, and she lingered on the forecourt, enjoying the cool, fresh air. Beside the garage was a neat square which looked newly swept. That must be where Dad had cleaned up the broken glass.

He had told Mum that the bottle had hit the forecourt, but Kirsty could see that it hadn't. The newly swept patch was against the garage wall, very close to the window. Much too close. A line of cold ran down her back.

She looked more carefully. She could see a grazed and damp patch on the wall – the bottle hadn't been quite empty, then. Dad didn't often drink beer at home, but she knew the smell. This was a beery smell, and there were still traces of brown glass on the ground.

Kirsty looked round at the broad road, the hills on either side, and their lonely house with the shed beside it. On the hill, the deer would be settling themselves for the night, safe in their herd. But Fawn needed protecting, and Mum was fragile, too. Kirsty had always felt safe here, but now she hurried to the house, wanting to close the front door and be locked in. Dad was just coming out with the phone in his hand.

"What's the bucket for, love?" he asked.

"Cat poo on the path," she said promptly. "I've cleared it up." That imaginary cat was coming in really useful. Dad nodded his approval.

"Good girl," he said. "Leave the door open, I'll be in in a minute."

"Dad," she said, "you know those men who drove away without paying?"

"Never mind about them," he said, too quickly and too sternly. All the same, she had to say this.

"Only I think that might be the car that knocked down the deer on the road, Dad, because—"

"Kirsty," he said firmly, "don't ask me about that car, or the people in it, or anything to do with it. Just don't. And don't mention it to anyone else. Anyone. Is that understood? Now off you go, I need to make a phone call."

So why wasn't he in the house, phoning from the landline? This must be a conversation he didn't want Mum to hear.

Kirsty felt as if a shadow had fallen across them. It had been like this when Auntie Sarah was ill, Mum and Dad taking care that she didn't hear their conversations. Finally, in those last two weeks, they had talked to her. *Auntie Sarah is very ill. Auntie Sarah is having a bad day today. Auntie Sarah is. . .*

There were still boxes of Auntie Sarah's stuff in the attic that hadn't been sorted out. Mum couldn't face it yet.

Don't think about that now. Come on. Clothes in the wash. This was becoming part of her routine now. She took a long, hot bath, washed her hair, felt a lot better for it, and went downstairs in her dressing gown with her hair still damp. Dad was on the settee with a car magazine in his hands.

Whatever had really been going on with the car, the noisy engine and the broken bottle, Dad wasn't going to tell her anything about it. All the same, she wanted to make him feel a bit better about things. He must be lonely, and she knew what that felt like. She bent over him and kissed the balding patch on the top of his head. Dad pulled a disgusted face.

"What a pong!" he exclaimed.

Kirsty felt her face turn scarlet. She'd washed thoroughly, even her hair, and changed her clothes. Did she still smell of deer?

"What did you have for tea?" he asked her.

"Lasagne," she said. "It was yummy."

"It was ninety per cent garlic!" he said. "Your breath stinks of it!"

Oh, she thought. *Garlic. That's OK.*

There were two policemen outside the garage the next morning, talking to Dad. Mal was there, too.

"Off to school, young Kirsty?" asked Mal.

No, I'm going on the Eurostar to Disneyland. "Yes," she said.

"Bit chilly for nearly June," he observed. "Where's your coat?"

"I don't need it," she answered. She had her warm school sweater and the cagoule.

"Have a good one!" he said, and turned to talk to the policemen. "There's some right little toerags around here," he told them. "I said to Andy, you want to get a solicitor's letter. You should do that, Andy, get a solicitor's letter."

Dad muttered something she couldn't hear, but she could guess what it was. Something like – *Shut up, Mal. Kirsty might hear you.*

It was getting harder to talk to Toby in the school playground. Georgia and Sally had noticed them spending a lot of time together, and now walked past them wrapping their arms round each other and gazing soppily into each other's eyes. It didn't actually do Toby and Kirsty any harm, but it was irritating and difficult to ignore.

Any chance to use the school computers was a great opportunity to learn more about caring for fawns, research their project, and have whispered conversations about Fawn. From a wildlife site on the internet, Toby found out that buttercups, grasses, rose petals and dandelions were all suitable for a fawn to eat. Kirsty couldn't help pointing out that she'd known all that for ages. All those plants grew near their school-bus stop, but they wondered what all those traffic fumes might do to them.

"We can get them from round my house," suggested Toby.

"It would look odd if we were going back to mine with bunches of dandelions," argued Kirsty. "We'll get all the food for Fawn from up the hill. We know it's safe from up there, because all the deer eat them."

"You're yawning again," said Toby with a glimmer of a smile.

"I can't help it," she said, and added, "Now you're doing it."

"That's because you did it first, and it's contagious," replied Toby, sounding know-it-all. "You know, all that about traffic fumes, we have to put that in the project. And pesticides."

"And broken glass," said Kirsty.

"Yes," agreed Toby. "There's loads of that about."

"There was some outside the garage last night, that's how I thought of it," she said, and told him about the bottle, and all that had happened. "Something's going on. Dad won't tell me, but I know somebody's getting at him."

"Any idea who?" he asked.

"You know about the car that nearly hit me and your dad?" she said. "I'm not supposed to tell you about them, but they drove away without paying and there's been trouble ever since. I'm pretty certain they're the ones who killed Fawn's mother, too, but even if I could prove it, I don't suppose it's a crime. Throwing things at the garage, I should think that's a crime, though."

"Your dad's talked to the police," Toby pointed out. "It'll be OK."

It might not be, thought Kirsty. *Not with Mum in the house and Fawn in the shed and both of them needing careful handling.* Kirsty sighed. She couldn't help looking forward to her next visit to Toby's house, where she wasn't expected to mother anyone – except maybe Rosemary and Mint, and they didn't count.

Feed Fawn, clean him, feed, clean. Clean everything, scrub bottles, make up bottles. Feed. Sometimes, when she closed her eyes at night, Kirsty could still see hay and bottles. She dreamed of Fawn, and woke in the night thinking she could hear him crying, the way Mum had thought she could hear Joseph. Sometimes, she would wake up not feeling sure where she was. One night she woke to feel a draught and wasn't even sure if she was inside the house or out of it – but it was only because Mum had wandered outside again, and left the door open. The next Saturday morning she would have slept in for hours if Toby hadn't called.

When Fawn had been fed and cleaned, Kirsty and Toby walked up the hill to watch the young deer. Some were bigger than Fawn, but all of them were nibbling at clover, wild pink-and-white rose petals, fresh, soft tips of brambles, and the feathery grasses that tickled their noses.

"Do you suppose Fawn can remember what other deer are like?" she asked Toby.

"Wouldn't think so," he said. "I suppose he'll soon remember when he gets back up here."

"They won't attack him, will they?"

"Of course not!" said Toby, but she wasn't sure if he really knew that.

They moved away from the deer feeding grounds, wanting to leave them in peace, and gathered handfuls of grasses. Kirsty pulled the fresh leaves from the tips of brambles and petals from the wild roses, and took some of the last bluebells for Mum, too. She left those on the sitting room window sill, where Mum would see them if she came down.

In the dark, cool shed, Toby sat down on what was left of the hay bale. Fawn trotted to see Kirsty and, as usual, hunted around her for bottles. When she held out grasses and flowers, he darted back in surprise. Kirsty offered clover in her fingers, and he sniffed suspiciously at it. *If he were a human*, she thought, *he'd pull a face.*

"He needs to see *you* eat it," said Toby from behind her. "Animals learn from watching their parents."

Kirsty kept her eyes on Fawn. She'd coped with all the messy stuff – but eating grass?

"I suppose I could pretend to eat it," she said, but she didn't need to. Fawn went on prodding and scenting at the clover. As they watched, he rooted about, explored the flowers with his nose and lips, and finally tasted, rolling the clover about with his tongue, swallowing it and reaching for more.

"He's eating!" she said.

"Wow!" whispered Toby. "Fantastic!"

"Good Fawn!" said Kirsty, and offered Fawn more clover. Watching him look after himself was even more exciting than giving him bottles. It said that he was alive and real, able to do things for himself. If Joseph had lived, she might have felt that way about him as he'd grown up.

"Are you all right?" asked Toby.

"Yeah, I was just thinking about something sad," she said.

"Then don't," he said. "Coming to our house today?"

She hesitated. Dad didn't seem too keen on her going to Toby's, but she liked it there. "Yes, but I won't stay long," she said.

Half term should have been a wonderful time, divided between caring for Fawn and going up to Hart Hill Farm whenever she could. But it didn't turn out that way. Mr and Mrs Gordon packed up the Land Rover and took Toby and Tessa to their grandparents' for a week.

"Well, I won't go away and leave you," she said to Fawn. She couldn't help being a bit jealous of Toby, but she was pleased, too, to be the one Fawn could rely on. When Toby came home, he stood in the dim shed and stared with amazement.

"He's bigger!" he exclaimed. "He can't have grown that much in a week!"

"Has he?" asked Kirsty. She hadn't noticed it, but now that Toby mentioned it she could see that Fawn was taller. He was growing up, becoming sturdier, no longer a baby, and she was proud of all she had done for him.

Over the following weeks, caring for Fawn became both easier and harder. It was easier because Kirsty became more efficient at making and cleaning bottles, and doing it when Mum and Dad were out of the way. Easier, too, because Fawn gradually came to want less milk and more wild food. She saw how he loved apple, bramble and clover. Dad seemed more and more wrapped up in the garage and less likely to notice what she was doing, and Mum was content to let her do as she liked. Mealtimes could be uncomfortably silent, as Dad always seemed wrapped in his own thoughts. The visit of the police and the words *solicitor's letter* stayed in Kirsty's mind, but she knew she shouldn't ask him about that.

Caring for Fawn grew harder, too, because he was

growing all the time. Every day, even if it poured with rain, she had to find him fresh leaves and branches. There was more mess to clean up, and as the summer grew hotter, it soon started to smell. The shed needed a thorough clean every day, either before or after school. He needed exercise and would gallop wildly about, training his muscles, learning speed. Watching him, Kirsty knew that he should be doing that on the hill with miles and miles of moorland to race through. There were tiny bobbles on his head where one day his antlers would grow.

It wouldn't have been so hard if Kirsty only had Fawn to look after, but there was Mum to think of, too. Kirsty tried to spend some time with her every day, even if it was only talking about school or watching something on television. When she went out gathering leaves she would bring wild flowers home for Mum, too. One day they talked about Auntie Sarah and Mum cried a bit, but then Dad came in and was worried. Later, he told Kirsty off for mentioning Auntie Sarah. "It upsets your mum," he said. But Kirsty knew that Mum loved to talk about Auntie Sarah, even if it did make her cry.

The summer term went on, the days were long and warm, but there was still homework to do. Apart from the wildlife project, Kirsty's work became hurried and careless. After she came back from cleaning the shed, she'd dabble her feet in a puddle to wash her trainers. That would have to do. In the evenings she would lovingly brush Mum's dark red hair and Fawn's soft brown coat, but her own hair only had a fight with a comb at bedtime. There were evenings when she felt too tired to go back to the house from the shed, and wished she could curl up in the hay against warm little Fawn. In the mornings, dragging herself from deep soft sleep, Kirsty would splash cold water on her face to wake herself up properly. If she watched television with Mum, she fell asleep. Sometimes, she'd be woken in the night by Mum wandering about, and at weekends she slept late. She couldn't help it. But on the days when she went to Toby's house she would go home first, change, wash, and give her hair a good brush because she so wanted Mrs Gordon to like her. They might think of her as Toby's scruffy friend, and that thought made her lower her head and squirm.

Her hands became scratched and itchy from the hay. Again and again she told herself that she could cope, and that it was only until Fawn was big and strong enough to be released, but she wasn't looking forward to that day. She knew it would come, but it seemed like a high black wall with nothing on the other side of it. While she had him, the loveliness of Fawn made up for everything else.

Whenever she could, Kirsty tried to make Mum laugh again. She would brush her hair over her face and put on sunglasses, or draw herself a moustache with eyeliner, and Mum would laugh, but not as freely and honestly as she had before, and Dad never laughed at all. He was either cross, or silent. If anything dropped through the letter box he'd sweep down to pick it up, though it would only be a charity collection bag or an advert for the Indian restaurant.

Though it was summer, and near the end of term, there were cool days when Kirsty wished she had her coat. On warmer days she'd go up to see what the wild deer were doing, imploring Mum to go with her, because surely anyone would feel happier from watching the deer? If only Mum would get out and breathe the fresh air and watch the deer – but Mum always said she was too tired, and she'd do it another day.

There was a daydream that Kirsty allowed herself sometimes, when she went to bed or when she was bored at school. It went something like Mum saying, "It really is time you had a decent new coat, ready for your new school," and Kirsty would say, "Yes, please!" and they'd go into town together and choose a coat – and why stop there? Mum might get her hair done, and buy herself something pretty. Kirsty imagined them going for a milkshake somewhere, and something to eat. It was only a daydream, but she could almost believe it.

But Fawn was real, growing taller and stronger and still as beautiful as ever. The hairbrush from Auntie Sarah grew dirty and greasy from grooming him, but this made it all the more precious. It connected her with both Fawn and Auntie Sarah. Brushing him was one of the things Kirsty loved, and he seemed to like it, too, standing absolutely still to be smoothed. She wished she had taken photographs of him from the day she first found him. Was his coat getting darker? She wasn't sure.

One Saturday morning, when Kirsty was due to go up to Toby's house, she lingered over Fawn. She had tried not to teach him that human company was normal, but sometimes, she couldn't help sitting on the floor or the remains of the hay bale, pressing her face against his neck and stroking him. She could talk freely to him when they were alone like this, without Toby. Fawn would stand perfectly still, apart from a flick of his ears and tail, while she told him about Auntie Sarah, and the places they used to go to together, and Mum.

"D'you think it would be different if Joseph had lived?" she asked him. "I don't suppose we'll ever know. Mum might still have got depressed. She tried some pills that the doctor gave her, but then she said they made her worse and gave them up, but she could have gone back, couldn't she? She could have said, 'Please, doctor, these don't work, can we try something different?' There must be loads of things they could have tried. There's the talky stuff, she never did that. I know it must be awful about Joseph, but, I mean, she's still got me. Your deer mum only thought about you. I suppose it's different for deer. She wasn't thinking about another little fawn, one that died or one that she might have one day; you were all she wanted. All right, my mum's not a deer, and people are more complicated. But if she can be sad that she doesn't have Joseph, can't she be happy that she's still got me? Am I not. . .?" She stopped. She didn't want to think this way. "Anyway, this is no good. I need to scrub up if I'm going to Toby's today."

Mrs Gordon set out a simple lunch – it was just sandwiches and fruit, but nicer than anything they ever had at home, and Kirsty glanced swiftly at Toby now and again to check on whether he had a second sandwich and how he ate an apple, because she didn't want to do anything that was bad manners. They'd finished eating and were sorting out charts and pictures when the rain started, and Mrs Gordon and Tessa came in from Tessa's riding lesson.

Kirsty was a bit shy of Tessa. Dressed for riding, she looked a lot older than she really was, and she usually seemed proud and bossy – but today she was in a good mood, taking an interest in what they were doing as she stood dangling her helmet. Toby called her "Tess-Mess" and she hit him, but it wasn't very hard and he didn't mind. There was a no-shoes-in-the-house rule, and Tessa in socks wasn't as scary as Tessa in riding boots.

Toby had obviously made up his mind to annoy his sister, and "Tess-Mess" was only the start of it. With his head bent innocently over his work, he made remarks about hobby horses, rocking horses, and dead horses, but Tessa didn't let any of it bother her. *If he were my little brother*, thought Kirsty, *I'd tip him out of that chair*. Tessa went into the kitchen for a glass of orange juice and asked Kirsty if she wanted one too. She even offered one to Toby.

"Tessa," asked Kirsty a bit shyly, when Tessa came back with the drinks, "what's it like having a little brother?"

Toby stopped pushing charts around and looked at her.

"Horrible," said Tessa. "Little brothers are a pain. They're noisy, they come into your bedroom, they make a mess. . ." She leaned on Toby's shoulder. "They show you up in front of your friends. If you haven't got one, you're very, very lucky!"

Toby was staring at her. "Is that what's the matter with your mum?" he asked. "Is she pregnant?"

"No!" snapped Kirsty. Toby shrank back.

"Ooh, scary scary Kirsty!" he said.

"Shut up, moron," said Tessa and tweaked his hair. Toby ignored her.

"What is it, though?" he asked Kirsty. "You're always saying that she's not well, but you never say what's the matter."

"It's none of your business, nosy," said Tessa. "She doesn't have to tell you, does she?"

They worked silently for a little longer. Tessa stood nearby, her phone in her hand, texting.

Finally, without looking up, Kirsty muttered, "It's depression, if you must know, OK?"

Toby put down his pen and sat back. "What's the matter with that?" he asked. "Loads of people have depression."

"She's not loads of people, she's my mum," Kirsty snapped back.

 148

Toby leaned his chin on his hands. "You sound like Tessa," he said.

Kirsty didn't answer. She had too much to think about. Should she have told Toby about Mum, and would he tell anyone else? What sort of a big sister would she have been to Joseph? Would Joseph have annoyed her on purpose, the way Toby did with Tessa? But there was no point in wondering about that. There was no Joseph.

Tessa went into the kitchen. When she was safely out of the way, Toby whispered, "How's he doing today?"

"Good," she whispered back. "Except that I wish we could exercise him, but we can't get him in and out without being seen, and he might run off and get lost."

"He might come back," Toby pointed out.

"He might not," she said. "Something might happen to him. He's not old enough to cope in the wild."

"We should tell—"

"No," she said firmly. By this time, she was so used to keeping Fawn a secret that she'd forgotten why it was important. She ran through a few reasons in her head.

Oh, yes. He might be shot for venison or put to sleep. And, whatever else might happen, I will be in big, big trouble if anyone finds out about him now, and just now:

Mum's ill and I have to look after her, and do the home stuff.

There's something the matter that Dad needs the police for.

149

Sally and Georgia are being a pain – two pains.

I haven't got Auntie Sarah.

I haven't got a coat.

So I don't need any more trouble just now. Certainly not the kind of trouble that would happen if we told anybody about the fawn, even nice Mrs Gordon.

"Kirsty," said Toby, not looking up from his work, "my mum's a solicitor. She works from home now, but she didn't always."

"Oh," murmured Kirsty. Dad had often said that the Gordons were "something to do with the law". She didn't know what a solicitor did, but she knew it was "something to do with the law".

"She's done loads of work for people who had depression," Toby went on. "She's represented people who got sacked because of it. She'd fight for them, to get them their jobs back, or make sure they got some money or something. She did a lot of really good stuff, so she could help your mum."

"My mum didn't have a job to be sacked from," said Kirsty. "She helped my dad, and he didn't sack her."

"No, but what I mean is, she's worked with loads of people who had depression," said Toby patiently. "She's used to it, she understands about it. She could go and call on your mum, if you like."

The thought of Mrs Gordon in their house made Kirsty want to duck. The piles of washing, the dust, the unwashed windows, the ring around the bath, the splashed cooker. And Mum would probably just curl up in the corner and hide. A bright stab of lightning flashed across the sky.

"Wow!" said Toby. They counted to five before the thunder banged above them.

"I have to go," said Kirsty, closing her books.

"Don't be silly, it'll be pouring in a minute!" Toby exclaimed.

She leaned closer, and whispered to him, "He'll be terrified. He's never been in a thunderstorm before. I have to go to him."

Toby stood up. "Then Mum or Dad will run you home."

"No, I'll be fine." She was already putting on the old cagoule.

"You haven't even got boots!" argued Toby. "You can't go in trainers!"

"Didn't know it was going to rain, did I?" said Kirsty. Long slashes of rain streaked the windows and bounced from the roof of the lambing shed. As Toby ran into the hall to call his mum, Kirsty took a deep breath, squared her shoulders, lowered her head and ran into the downpour, but she was barely past the gate when she heard an engine. A car drew up, the windscreen wipers swishing, and Mrs Gordon opened the door.

"Get in, Kirsty!" she called. "I can't let you go home alone in this! What would your parents say?"

Don't suppose they'd notice, thought Kirsty as she slipped gratefully into the passenger seat. "Thanks," she said. "I would have walked, I don't mind getting wet."

"Nonsense!" said Mrs Gordon firmly, and chatted

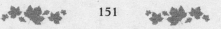

151

about how hard it was to get Tess and Toby to help about the house, the sort of things mothers always talk about. She was so easy to get on with that Kirsty dared to say, "Toby said you're a solicitor."

"Yes, I am," she said.

"Then—" Kirsty hesitated, then asked her question. "Please can you tell me, what's a solicitor's letter?" As soon as she'd asked it, she felt stupid, and blushed. A solicitor's letter was a letter written by a solicitor, obviously! But Mrs Gordon didn't seem to think it was a silly question at all.

"A solicitor's letter?" she repeated. "Where have you heard about that?"

"Somebody said it to my dad," she confided. "Something about getting a solicitor's letter."

"It may be that somebody owes him money," said Mrs Gordon as she parked outside the house. "If he's been asking a customer for payment and they won't pay. If he can't get any money out of them, he might ask a solicitor to write a letter saying, 'If you don't pay, we're going to take you to court and sue you.' Or it could be that somebody's being a nuisance. A solicitor's letter can scare people into paying up or calming down. It doesn't always work, but it very often does." As she parked, she turned to Kirsty. "Tell your dad to give me a call, Kirsty, if anything's bothering him."

Kirsty was about to answer, but at that moment she saw something that made her heart race.

"Thank you very much, Mrs Gordon," she said politely, and scrambled out of the car. She let herself into the house with her own key, but as soon as Mrs Gordon's car was out of the way she dashed through the rain to the shed. The door stood wide open.

Chapter Ten

In the rain and heavy sky, the shed was gloomy. Mum stood a little inside the door, shivering. Kirsty looked past her into the shadows.

No Fawn.

She'd have to get Mum out first, quickly and quietly, and then she'd be able to look for him. He might still be in the shed. *Oh, please, Fawn, be in the shed. Please, just let him still be in the shed. Please please don't let him hear my voice and come to me, at least not while Mum's around. Please please keep him safe.*

"Mum?" Kirsty said softly. Mum jumped, with a little gasp. "Did the storm bother you?"

"Storm," repeated Mum vaguely, then finally turned to her. "I heard it, Kirsty, I really did. That crying. I heard it again."

"It'll be that cat," said Kirsty. "It must be hanging around again. Come in, Mum, you're soaked, and it's cold in here. Come and get warm."

Kirsty urged her mother out of the shed and closed the door behind her. She led Mum back to the house, put on the gas fire to warm her and made her a cup of tea, all the time thinking of Fawn.

"It was crying," said Mum vaguely. "Poor little thing."

"It was just mewing, like all cats do," said Kirsty. "Now you stay there, and I'll go and make sure it's all right. Get warm, drink your tea. I'll be back in a minute."

She took the torch and splashed through the rain to the shed. The rain pounding on the roof was so loud, she was afraid it would drown out her voice. She took a handful of grass from the floor and held it out.

"Fawn?" she said. *Be there, oh, please, please, be there.*

Silence.

She shone the light into a stall. Nothing there. Nothing in the next one. Her stomach felt queasy with fear. She had to hold the torch with both hands to keep it still.

In the last stall of the row, in the furthest corner, she found him. He stood pressed into the angle of the wall, shivering, with his head down. When he saw her he took a step towards her, sniffing and licking at her hands.

The tight knot of fear twisted deep in Kirsty's stomach. Something was wrong. He was either hurt or

155

terrified, and she hoped he was only terrified, but he might have injured himself as he bolted into the corner. She let Fawn nuzzle her hand and found his nose was cold and wet, as it should be, like a dog's nose. He ate the grass she held out to him, and the knot inside her slackened a little. Not hurt, then, just frightened. She knew what to do about that.

"Shush, now," she said, smoothing his long, warm neck. "Did the lightning scare you? That's why I came home. Or were you scared because of my mum coming in? Good Fawn. Always hide from people. It's what your mum would have taught you. Run and hide. There, there, now. It's all right."

Under her steady hand, Fawn became calm. She could feel the too-tight muscles relaxing under her hand. His trembling stopped.

"That's better," she said. "Now, you stay here, little fawn, and stay quiet. You see what happens when you bleat? Mum mustn't know about you."

Into her mind flashed the picture of Mum, standing bewildered in the stable doorway as the rain hammered the roof. She turned away so quickly that Fawn flinched.

"Sorry," she said. "I have to go and make sure that Mum's all right, otherwise she might wander in here again. I didn't know she had a key. You be good. I'll come back."

As she left, locking the door behind her and pocketing Mum's key, something seemed to bubble up inside her. If Mum was going to be ill, why didn't she just curl up on the settee or in bed and stay put! *Just stay there, Mum, don't make things worse than they already are, and leave my secret alone!*

The power of her anger terrified Kirsty. She was scared, that was all, scared for Fawn, and so now she was taking it out on Mum. Fawn's tension had released under her gentling hand, and she needed her own anxiety to fall away too. Fawn was still safe and secret, Mum was indoors, nothing terrible had happened, and she had Mum's key. She was trembling, as Fawn had trembled. But for Kirsty, there was nobody to smooth and soothe her with a kind hand.

"Quiet, Kirsty," she told herself gently, leaning against the shed door. "You're all right. All you have to do now is take a deep breath" – so she did – "and go and see what Mum's doing."

At least the rain was stopping, and there was blue sky above. Kirsty suddenly realized how wet she was, and ran for the house.

"Your cup of tea was getting cold, Kirsty," said Mum. "I'll give it a few seconds in the microwave." This was encouraging, until she crossed the kitchen and Kirsty heard the water squelch in her shoes.

"Mum, you're still soaked," she said. "Your feet are wet. Take those shoes off. Get changed, and I'll find a towel for your hair."

"It doesn't matter," said Mum.

"Yes it does!" said Kirsty. "You being warm and dry matters. I don't want you to have wet feet."

She ushered Mum upstairs, remembering when

Mum used to do this for her on rainy days. There had been one winter afternoon when the rain had pelted down so hard that she'd got soaked to the skin just running from the bus to the front door, and Mum and Auntie Sarah had bustled her up the stairs, run her a bath, and warmed a big fluffy towel for her as if she were a princess and they both wanted to be her favourite maid. She smiled at the memory.

"What was in the shed?" asked Mum. "Was it that cat? Is it all right?"

Kirsty wondered how long she could keep up this imaginary cat. "The cat's fine," she said. "It ran away home."

It was best to say this, otherwise Mum might go out looking for the wretched thing. Kirsty sorted out a towel for Mum's hair, made Fawn's bottle, and hid it in her wardrobe. The rain had stopped and she slipped back into the sitting room and, for fresh air, opened a window. Suddenly she heard Dad and Mal talking outside.

"There's not enough police on the beat these days," Mal was saying. "It's not right. They seem to think they've got more important things to do than look after us. They're too busy to catch criminals these days."

"I took a picture of the graffiti before I scrubbed it off," said Dad. "It must have been done this morning when I was in the house – it wasn't dry when I got to it. But they said I still couldn't prove who did it. I told them, I've had two guys who ran off without paying, I've demanded payment, and now I'm getting threatening phone calls and letters. . ."

"And broken glass," added Mal.

". . .broken glass, and I reckon they were aiming for the window," Dad continued.

"That's dead nasty, that, Andy," said Mal.

"I spoke to the sergeant over the phone today," said Dad, "and he's coming over to meet me. He's coming in a plain car and I said to him to go to the garage, not the house."

"You don't want Debbie knowing about all this trouble, then?" asked Mal.

"I don't want Kirsty knowing, either," said Dad. Kirsty stepped a little way back from the window. They hadn't seen her, and she didn't want them to.

So, as she had guessed, the blue car men had been threatening the garage. It was one more thing to cope with, but how could she help if Dad wouldn't let her? Perhaps she couldn't help at all. She was already busy looking after Mum and Fawn. Oh, and herself.

Finally, when Mal had gone home and Dad was doing the last odds and ends of tidying up in the office, she had the chance to slip out to the shed. They'd been talking so long that the bottle would have cooled down. On the side of the garage was a freshly scrubbed rectangle where traces of paint still showed, and she hoped Mum wouldn't see that.

Fawn had calmed down completely when she came in. He was grazing on some clover and leaves and trotted over calmly, trustingly, for his milk, not rushing at her. He must be getting used to the food from the hill. That was good, because it brought them a step nearer to setting him free. But whenever that day came, it would be too soon. Kirsty imagined taking him up to the hill and leaving him there to run to his heart's content, to drink from the streams and graze in the shade with the herd. That would be a proud, beautiful, joyful day. But it would break her heart, so she mustn't think about it yet.

Kirsty was tired, very tired, long before she finished cleaning the floor. When it was all done, and the smelly straw and poo had been dumped in the wood, she sat down on a heap of clean hay. She'd have five minutes just to enjoy watching Fawn before going back into the house. She watched him saunter round the shed, nosing at leaves and grass stems, tasting a little before he came to stand beside her. Slowly, he curled his front legs beneath him as he settled down.

She watched him, looking yet again at the shape of his head where one day he would grow antlers, at the line along his back and his clear white patches. She smiled, and looked away from him at the length of the stable, thinking how small a space it was for him to run around.

Something touched her leg. Slowly, not to alarm him, she turned her head.

Fawn's nose was against her thigh. He stretched out his neck, seemed to sigh, and made himself comfortable with his head in her lap.

She could barely breathe for happiness. She wanted time to stop. There could be nothing more perfect in life than this moment and she wanted to keep it inside her for ever, sitting still with Fawn lying at her feet, resting his head in her lap. Never mind what she should or should not do. She stroked him gently and he lay still, gazing serenely ahead of him.

"Thank you," she said.

After the day of the thunderstorm, the weather stayed cool and fresh for a week. Fawn took less milk and more grass, leaves and apples – there was never any shortage of apples at Toby's house, and they could help themselves. The only problem was exercise, and there was nothing they could do about that.

Kirsty still tried to make Mum laugh. Sometimes it worked. There was still time, at weekends, to go up the hill with Toby and observe the deer. A fawn might be hiding in the grass close by, and they wouldn't want to disturb it. Now and again they would see the fawns playing and racing about the hillside.

"I should show Mum how they do that," said Kirsty.

"It's called frolicking," said Toby.

"*Frolicking!*" repeated Kirsty, and began to giggle. It was one of those words which was just funny, whatever it meant. It sounded silly and a bit rude, too.

"Yeah, that's what it is," said Toby, grinning. "In those old-fashioned books my grandma has in her house, lambs frolic. Children frolic. It means – what's the matter with you?"

Kirsty had rolled on her back laughing. "Frolic!" she repeated, and could hardly get the word out. She hurt with laughing. Toby was laughing, too.

"It means what the fawns do," he said. "All that jumping about and skipping, all that bouncy stuff," said Toby. "They're having a frolic." And as the word made her laugh so much, he repeated, "Frolic, frolic. Kirsty, you are getting much too frolicky. Stop frolicking at once. Are you having a frolic?"

Kirsty got up and dusted herself down. After several attempts to speak, she managed to get the words out.

"I'm going to see Mum. I want to tell her about frolicking."

"Will she be up yet?"

"Who cares?"

She ran down the hill with Toby following, and found Mum in the kitchen.

"Mum, we've been watching the fawns," she said. "Look, they do this thing, and it's called. . ." She doubled over with laughter again, and couldn't get the word out, so she went on, "They do this. . ."

She held her arms out like forelegs and bounced round the kitchen and down the hall, bucking and springing as the fawns did. "They do it like this. Toby says it's called. . ."

Mum was laughing, and her whole face had brightened. Kirsty ran and hugged her. It was like watching ice thaw, or the sun coming out from behind the clouds, and shining.

"Frolicking," said Toby behind her. "In the old books, they called it frolicking."

Kirsty had forgotten he was there. Toby stood behind her in the hall, looking – well, looking at home. He was relaxed, and smiling. Posh Toby Gordon was standing in the shabby hall, with a cobweb above his head and Dad's oily jeans drying over the radiator, and it didn't matter.

"Come up the hill and see them, Mum," urged Kirsty.

"Maybe another day, sweetheart," said Mum. "I'm a bit tired today."

The sun had disappeared behind a cloud again. Perhaps it was too much, too soon. But Kirsty felt better. She knew that the sun was still there, and that it would appear again.

"I'm going to Toby's house after school," Kirsty said to Dad a few days later, at breakfast time. Dad put down his mug of tea, folded his hands, and looked across the table at her with his eyebrows raised. Kirsty corrected herself.

"May I go to Toby's after school, please, Dad?"

"Is it for your wildlife project? I suppose so, then. But don't stay late; don't outstay your welcome."

Kirsty very nearly asked him what was so wrong about Toby, or his family, or her going to see them. She didn't ask, because she was sure she wouldn't get

163

a proper answer. Anyway, she had a feeling that she understood.

Dad didn't want her to go to Hart Hill in the same way that she hadn't wanted to bring Toby into their house. As Dad saw it, the people at Hart Hill Farm were Something To Do With the Law, lived in a place too big for them, kept sheep for fun and had a daughter who went riding. Tessa went to a private school, and so would Toby, next year. The Gordons weren't like the Weavers. Dad was something to do with getting engine oil all over your hands. They lived in a dingy, messy little house with no garden, just a yard and the garage and a heap of tyres, and the falling-apart car. The way Dad saw it, there was much more than a main road between one family and the other.

All the same, she went up to Toby's house that evening. At Hart Hill Farm sweet peas curled round the front door, almost too pretty with their pastel colours and graceful petals. In the warm evening after a brief shower of rain, they left perfume in the air. Mrs Gordon stood among them, snipping the long stems and laying them down in a basket.

"Hello, Kirsty!" she called. "I have to keep doing this. The more you cut them, the more they grow. Toby's at the computer."

Toby had found some charts about chemicals in streams from lead mines. It sounded almost as boring as the stuff Dad and Mal said when they talked about engines, but she supposed it would impress the teachers. Nobody was near enough to hear them discussing Fawn, but they talked in whispers, just in case.

"Has your mum heard him again?" asked Toby.

"Not since the storm," Kirsty whispered back, her head bent over the columns of figures on the desk. "He doesn't mew and bleat as much as he did. I think it's because he's not so hungry all the time."

"Maybe he's found out that it doesn't work," said Toby. "You feed him when you can, not when he bleats. That's what you wanted him to learn, isn't it?"

It was. All the same, Kirsty didn't like the idea of Fawn crying for her, and giving up because she didn't come.

"He knows he mustn't draw attention to himself," she said. "That's what he'll need when he goes back to the wild."

"So when are we letting him go?" asked Toby.

We? thought Kirsty, bending her head over her work. *Excuse me?* But out loud she only said "Soon," and changed the subject. After a lot of work, a meal of pizza, salad and warm crusty bread, and helping to clear up in the kitchen, Kirsty said she'd have to go home.

"I'll drive you home," said Mrs Gordon. She wrapped some sweet peas in tissue paper and put them in the car with a pile of glossy magazines tied up with garden string. A green hoodie, which Kirsty thought must be Tessa's, lay on the back seat.

"Those magazines and the flowers are for your mum," said Mrs Gordon as they got into the car.

165

"Thank you!" cried Kirsty, and the cry came straight from her heart. It would be like bringing summer into the house. "She loves flowers. She used to do lovely flower drawings before. . ." She stopped. She had nearly said "before the depression", but stopped herself. "Before she wasn't very well," she said lamely.

"Oh, and that green hoodie," said Mrs Gordon, with her eyes on the road, "will that be any use to you? It was Tessa's, and she'd hardly worn it before she grew six inches overnight. It needs a good home."

"Thank you – thank you very much!" said Kirsty, who suddenly felt she couldn't say "thank you" enough. "And for the things for Mum, too!"

"You're welcome. Would she like visitors?" asked Mrs Gordon.

"Oh, no!" said Kirsty, so quickly that she was afraid it might seem rude. "I mean, it's very kind of you, thank you, but – um – she doesn't really see anyone."

Mrs Gordon didn't seem to think there was anything strange about this, or ask her why Mum didn't "really see" people. "Never mind," she said. "Will you just let her know that I can call by if ever she'd like company? Or she could come up to Hart Hill, if she likes. You've got our number, haven't you?"

Oh, I wish, thought Kirsty as she nodded. It would do Mum the world of good to have someone as warm and kind as Mrs Gordon to talk to. But Mum wouldn't want to see Mrs Gordon, and Kirsty didn't want Mrs Gordon to see the house, and she couldn't get Mum to go to the doctor, let alone Hart Hill. She couldn't see how she'd ever get Mum and Mrs Gordon into the same place.

As the car reached the bottom of the hill, something deep inside Kirsty rebelled against all the half truths and secrecy. She long to tell everything, to take a deep breath and say – *Please, Mrs Gordon, please don't be cross, but I rescued a baby fawn – and I can't tell Mum and Dad – and please will you help me, and the fawn, and promise you won't let anyone shoot him or have him for venison. . .*

No, it was too dangerous. Perhaps she could just say, "Mum's depressed." She could even say, "Somebody's making trouble for my dad, we've had broken glass and graffiti. . ."

The car slowed to a halt at the front door. Kirsty felt the colour rise in her face.

"Thank you, Mrs Gordon," she said, and found that her voice was shaky. "And thank you for the hoodie." With one hand already on the door handle, she struggled to find words.

"Mrs Gordon. . ."

It was no more than a tight little whisper. Shyness and awkwardness silenced her. She tried again, while Mrs Gordon sat patiently, waiting for her to say what she wanted to say. But Kirsty's voice had deserted her. All she could do was throw her arms round Toby's mum and hug her tightly, feeling the fresh softness of the cardigan against her face, the cool round pearls digging into her forehead, and the arms that wrapped comfortingly round her and gently patted her shoulder the way nobody else did any more. Then she reached again for the door handle, bending to hide her scarlet face.

"Don't forget these!" called Mrs Gordon, holding out the flowers and magazines. Kirsty stammered another thank you, grabbed them, and ran into the house.

When Kirsty thought later of the following few days, two moments stood out. One was lovely. One was terrible.

It was a day which started quite normally – or, at least, it was Kirsty's sort of normal, which meant getting up early to make up a bottle, feed Fawn in secret and hang up last night's washing before going to school, then avoiding Georgia and Sally, who were getting worse. If they saw her anywhere near Toby they'd put their arms round each other and gasp, "Darling Kirsty! Oh, darling Toby!" The newest thing was that if her clothes were crumpled, her socks falling down, or her hair in more of a mess than usual, they would point and giggle. *I must ask Mum to teach me to iron properly*, thought Kirsty. But that wasn't the worst thing.

She had done her best to keep herself clean, so nobody would guess that she was looking after an animal. From the way Georgia and Sally held their noses and flapped their hands when they saw her, she hadn't tried hard enough. It wasn't enough for them just to do that, either. They had to finish it with a noise, a snort or a snigger of a giggle from Sally and a high-pitched shriek from Georgia that made Kirsty wince to hear it. As far as possible, she kept out of their way. She would ask herself what use Sally and Georgia were. *I look after my Mum, I saved a fawn's life and I'm looking after him, and what are those two good for?* As the end of the school day grew nearer, she would watch the clock, eager to get out of school quickly before they could point and giggle any more, and even more eager to get home to Fawn. But on this day, Mrs Baines stopped her before she could leave.

"Kirsty," she said in a voice you couldn't argue with, "you seem to find it hard to concentrate just now."

"Sorry, miss," she said, looking at the floor.

"Is anyone being unkind to you? Anyone at school?"

Kirsty glanced up, then down again. "Please, miss, I have to catch the bus," she said. It was bad enough being humiliated by bullies without having to talk about it too.

"Is everything all right at home?"

Kirsty didn't answer. She mustn't talk about home, however much she wanted to. She couldn't hug Mrs Baines the way she'd hugged Mrs Gordon. And she really must catch the bus.

"Yes, miss," she said. "It's all fine." It was such an enormous lie, she felt it would swallow her. Her heart longed for wide-eyed Fawn, who didn't know about school and didn't care, who never asked questions. Fawn, who was uncomplicated, and beautiful, and secret.

"Off you go, then," said Mrs Baines at last, and Kirsty hurried away to find Toby waiting for her. To a background of "Darling Toby! Darling Kirsty!" from Georgia and Sarah, they walked quickly to the bus stop.

"Have you said anything to Mrs Baines?" she accused him.

"About what?"

"About me." She nodded towards Georgia and Sally. "About those two."

"No!" he said, so indignantly that she knew he was telling the truth. "I wish I had done, though."

Kirsty shrugged. All she wanted was to get home to Fawn as quickly as possible.

Kirsty got home to find the "back in thirty minutes" sign on the garage door, and Mum asleep in an armchair. She was about to tiptoe out when something on the table made her look again. She caught her breath.

On the table were the sweet peas from Mrs Gordon, in a vase of water, as Kirsty had left them. Beside them, a magazine lay open at a picture from a flower show. And in front of them, spread across the table, were old envelopes with pencil sketches on the backs. There were rough drawings of the sweet peas. A fallen petal, its detail of light and dark carefully shaded in. A half-finished sketch of a rose. An outline of a lily.

They were all unfinished apart from the small, perfect petal. Happiness rose in Kirsty like bubbles. The moment was magical.

She dashed upstairs, found coloured pencils and paper, and left them with the drawings and magazines, where Mum would find them. Then she made up a bottle. Even though Fawn was eating more solid food now, he still seemed to want milk. She ran to the shed.

"Mum's drawing again!" she said as he took the bottle and tugged hard at it. "You're magic! You make good things happen! Hey, settle down, don't drink so quickly." Fawn was good at listening, never interrupting or arguing. She stroked his neck. "I think it's going to be all right. It'll be summer holidays soon, so I won't have Georgia and Sally hanging round any more. And maybe you'll be able to go back to the hills."

She imagined mornings and evenings with no bottles, no mess to clean up, no secrecy. No more having to hide bottles under her bed. No Fawn in the shed. What would she do?

"I'll still come to see you," Kirsty said, easing the empty bottle from his mouth and stroking his neck. She knelt and looked into his eyes. "But you mustn't come running over to see if I've brought a bottle, because I won't. You'll be too grown up for bottles. And if two very silly girl fawns called Sally and Georgia follow you around, just chase them away. Good boy."

It was hard to leave him so she stayed, looking into the large, gentle eyes, watching his wide ears twitch at every sound. Every moment with him was precious and beautiful. Behind them, on the main road, a siren blared, and Fawn bolted into the shelter of a stall.

"Good," she whispered. He hadn't lost the instinct

to hide, but he'd hidden in a corner. "On the hill, you'd have to keep running. If you hide in corners you could get trapped." *You'd be trapped and I wouldn't be there to help you.* She didn't like that idea. "You know what I should do now? I should see if I can get Mum to come for a walk up the hill to see your friends. She might want to draw them, too. It's a beautiful day, she might just come."

Fawn gave a little shake of his head.

"I know, I know," said Kirsty, "if anyone's going up that hill, it should be you. But not yet, little one, not yet. Not while you still need bottles. And me."

In spite of all Kirsty's efforts, Mum wouldn't go with her up the hill that day, so the following Saturday afternoon Kirsty refused to help with hanging out the washing – "Not unless you come with me for a deer watching walk up the hill, Mum." She hid the washing basket, then ran away with it, and finally Mum laughed and agreed.

"Now," insisted Kirsty. "Before you can change your mind. You promised."

Knowing how easily Mum could grow tired or distracted, Kirsty took care to keep her noticing things all the time as they climbed the hill. "There's a really good view from round the next corner, Mum," she said, and then later, "Further up here, that's where the wood anemones grow." Finally, after a lot of encouraging, coaxing, urging and waiting, they reached the wood by the clearing.

"Be very, very quiet," whispered Kirsty. "And watch!"

They watched. Mum stood wide-eyed like a small child, saying nothing. A buck prowled past, his antlers carried high. The does grazed idly round the hillside, sure of themselves, knowing that they were where they belonged. In the distance, two fawns chased each other, wheeling and leaping the way Fawn did in the shed.

Mum reached into her pocket for a scrappy little notebook and a pencil, and began to sketch. Kirsty knelt down in the grass. There were flies on the hill and the deer would whisk sharply round to bite them, or scratch at them with their hind legs. Fawn would love it out here. He'd feel the wet grass on his legs. If it rained, he'd copy the rest of the herd and hide among the trees, or she hoped he would.

She looked over Mum's shoulders at the sketches. She'd drawn the head of a stag looking up and sniffing the air. A fawn's hoof with grass round it. A doe, bending her head to graze.

"They must feel lovely to touch," said Mum.

"They. . ." began Kirsty, and just managed to stop herself from saying "they do". "They must be," she finished. "The young ones especially." Mum finally folded up her notebook and they made their way back down the hill, talking about the deer, the wildlife and the heather track, while Kirsty told Mum how good her sketches were, and finally Mum, who didn't seem to be listening, said, "I can smell burning, can you?"

Kirsty was about to say that Mum was imagining it

when she, too, caught a bitter tang of smoke on the air. She hurried ahead. Whatever was wrong, Mum mustn't see it first. From somewhere, somewhere much too near home, thick dark smoke curled upwards.

Kirsty ran.

Chapter Eleven

The billows of smoke were so dark and dense that Kirsty couldn't see where they were coming from, but she could guess. That spot, near the garage, was where the old stripped-down car stood on its piles of bricks. Before she was near it, her eyes were stinging.

Her first thought was to throw water on it, but then she remembered something about not using water on some kinds of fires, so she grabbed Mum's hand and ran with her to the house. She stretched out for the phone, but Mum already had her mobile in her hand and was pressing the nine key with shaking hands.

Where was Dad? Running in a wide circle, holding up one hand to shield her face from the heat and choking smoke, Kirsty reached the garage. "Back in thirty minutes" read the sign on the locked door.

There were fire blankets in the garage and the office, but she couldn't get to those. There was one in the kitchen – no good; she wouldn't be able to get near enough to the fire to use it. But the smoke was nowhere near the shed, so Fawn was safe. She ran back to the house, where Mum was still talking to the Fire Service.

"Tell them we're on the main road!" called Kirsty. Mum hesitated, looked flustered, and handed her the phone.

"It's Weaver's Garage on the main road," said Kirsty hurriedly. "The smoke's really black and thick and if it blows over the road the drivers won't be able to see anything, so it's really dangerous." She handed the phone back to Mum, who was still shaking, and hugged her. "That should hurry them. Well done, Mum."

"Where's your dad?" asked Mum. Her voice shook.

"He's put up the 'back in thirty' sign," Kirsty told her. "So he's probably gone to fetch spare parts or something. We're both all right. Nobody's in danger."

Unless we've inhaled toxic smoke, she thought. *And unless Fawn's inhaled the smoke, and then I'd have to get a vet and there's no way he could stay secret after that, and we can't pay for a vet.* Soon the strident siren of a fire engine grew louder, and nearer, and firemen came running across the forecourt. By the time Dad came back even the smouldering had stopped, but the air was still dark and bitter with smoke.

Kirsty waited and watched as the firemen, gathering round the car, made sure every last spark had died and the ashes and blackened metal had cooled. One of the crew – Kirsty thought he might be in charge – stood talking to Dad. Both of them were grimy with soot. *Good thing Dad's wearing overalls.* Presently, a police car arrived, too. Dad strode towards her. *He's going to tell me to go inside and look after Mum*, thought Kirsty, but she was wrong.

"The police want to talk to you," he said. "In the office." His voice was so grim that Kirsty was sure she was in trouble – *They don't think I started the fire, do they?* She was ready to argue, but the red-faced police officer, sitting in the only chair, stood up and smiled kindly down at her.

"You're not in trouble, love," he said. "I just need to ask you some questions. Was it you who called 999?"

"No, that was my mum," she said. "But I was there." The officer looked across her at Dad, who shook his head very slightly.

"You'd best talk to Kirsty," he said. "Her mum's not well."

So there were questions, often the same question over and over again, for Kirsty to answer – what time did they go out, when did they get back, could she be sure of those times, had she seen anyone (he asked that one at least three times), had she seen anything unusual, had anyone been hanging about? Finally, he thanked her, and told her she'd done all the right things, and then they both told her to look after her mum. *What do you think I'm always doing?* thought Kirsty. And as he opened the door for her, Dad said,

"What was your mum doing, wandering off up the hill?"

"She didn't wander off," explained Kirsty patiently. "We went up the hill together. She wasn't in danger."

"Not a word to her about anything the police have said, mind," Dad warned her. "Or anything you've heard from me. Just don't say anything."

As if I had anything to say! thought Kirsty. *Nobody tells me anything!*

In the house, Kirsty caught a glimpse of herself in the mirror and looked again in shock. Her face was even grimier than Dad's. She rubbed at the soot, and only managed to spread it about. Mum was looking out from the sitting room window.

"There are police all round that old car," she said. "I wonder what they're looking for?"

"Nothing," said Kirsty carelessly. "It's just what they have to do. They have to do tests and checks and stuff."

"So what started the fire?" asked Mum, worrying at the question as if she were asking herself, not Kirsty. "It couldn't have just happened by accident. What was it?"

Kirsty honestly said that she didn't know. She had her own ideas about it, especially with the police showing so much interest, but she wasn't going to tell Mum, who was biting her lip and fidgeting. Dad came in, washed his hands, and left black marks all over the towel.

"There must have been a spark from something," he said. "Maybe there's been an oily rag left in there, and someone's been a bit careless with a match. Probably Mal. I'll speak to him."

But Mal hasn't been here all day, thought Kirsty. She looked at Dad, who raised his eyebrows at her to tell her to keep quiet.

As soon as Mum had left the room, she said, "Dad, please tell me what's going on."

"Nothing I can't cope with, love," he said.

"But. . ." She wondered how to put this. Should she say to him – *Dad, I know Mal wasn't here today? What about that time when you found the broken glass? And that graffiti? What if they come back? This time it was the old car, but next time it could be. . .*

Dad put an arm round her shoulders and squeezed her. "It's going to be all right, little love," he said. "Don't you worry."

But, of course, she did.

In the shed, Fawn seemed uneasy, too. The smell of the smoke had reached him, and he had taken shelter in the furthest corner again. Kirsty wondered what it was like, being locked into a building, not able to get out. She shuddered. It wasn't a pleasant thought.

"I wouldn't like being shut in, Fawn," she said as she shook the bottle. "And I'm an animal that lives in a house, not like you, born on the hill. Still, it's the only thing to do just now."

He came calmly for his bottle, finishing it in

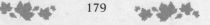

179

seconds. She offered him leaves and branches she had brought him in the morning, and though they were already looking droopy, he ate them. She hadn't brought any fresh ones, in case they tasted of smoke, but she'd taken a carrot and an apple from the kitchen and watched him munch messily at them.

Then she took the hairbrush and smoothed him down.

"Good Fawn," she said gently, with every sweep of the brush. "Good Fawn."

He stood perfectly still, as if it were a great treat and he wanted to make the most of every second of it. "Good Fawn," she repeated as she brushed, until her anxiety had faded away, she felt tired and very peaceful, and the fire seemed a long time ago. She put down the brush and stroked him gently as he settled himself down in the hay.

"Do you feel better for that, Fawn?" she asked him. "Because I do. You're so good for me. You're my hero. My bright light. My – what's that word for a charm or something? Talisman." As usual, she remembered too late that she shouldn't talk to him so much, so instead she sat beside him, sharing his stillness, his quietness and peace. But at last she had to go, reluctantly, back through the smoke-smelling yard to the house where nobody told the whole truth.

The next day it was a relief to get away from the house and the garage. At Toby's house, when they were sitting at a table designing the cover of their project, Kirsty told him about the fire.

"The police kept asking me if I'd seen anything," she said. "I wish I had. Dad and I both know it wasn't an accident, and it just makes me wonder. . ." She lowered her voice. It was as if she could make the worst happen by talking too loudly about it. "What if something happens at the shed?"

Toby stopped drawing and considered this very carefully, like working out the answer to a riddle or a maths problem. Then he said, "If it's the same people, they've only attacked the garage up to now. The shed's well away from it, so Fawn should be safe. But the sooner we get him out, the better."

"You just said he'd be safe," objected Kirsty.

"I can't say he'd be *completely* safe," said Toby, being annoyingly sensible. "Mum and Dad would help, if we only told them. They'd love to help. They wouldn't mind paying for anything."

Kirsty shook her head. "No way," she said. "If we told one lot of parents we'd have to tell the other. Dad would go off like a bomb."

"We have to be ready to let him go," insisted Toby. "If there's rough stuff going on at your place, Fawn will be a lot safer on the hill."

"He's too young!" she said. "He still needs mothering, and milk, and he's not going to get those on the hill, is he?"

Toby had picked up a bit of orange twine and was trying to make it look like tangled fishing line. He twisted and turned it, and finally said, "It's like this. You can never know that he'll be completely safe *anywhere.* The wild isn't safe, not for anyone. There's no regular food, and he could get hurt jumping a fence or something. But then he could hurt himself when he's leaping about in the shed. So nothing's completely safe."

"Well, thanks a lot," Kirsty muttered crossly, but she knew he was right. She had always known that looking after a fawn would be difficult. She just hadn't realized it would be this complicated. When it was time for her to go, Mrs Gordon gave her more flowers and magazines for Mum.

"Mum sketched the flowers last time," she said as she got out of the car, and wondered if Mrs Gordon would understand how important that was. Perhaps she did. This time, there was a card among the flowers, with a phone number and a note:

Thanks for letting Kirsty come – fancy getting together for a coffee? – Kate G

Mum was asleep, but on the table were scattered pencil drawings of sweet peas and roses, with the rose petals shaded in reds and pinks. Green leaves curled from behind them. Perhaps Mum would take up Mrs Gordon's invitation. Kirsty very much hoped so.

Monday morning started very, very badly. Kirsty went to the shed wearing her school uniform. She was thinking about releasing Fawn, and when to do it, and how he'd cope in the wild, so she wasn't really concentrating on what she was doing and didn't notice the patch of deer pee on the floor until she'd slipped in it and bumped down hard. Alarmed at the sudden movement and Kirsty's shriek of "Ow!", Fawn flinched and, as usual, hid in a corner. Kirsty scrambled to her feet, reminding herself that this was a good sign. If he'd come to see what was the matter with her it would be very sweet, very like Snow White in the forest, but it would mean he was too tame.

"Good Fawn," she muttered as she twisted round to inspect the back of her skirt. Fortunately she had another one, so she went back to her bedroom to change, but when she picked up the spare skirt, she pulled a face. It smelled of stale smoke. Too late, she remembered that it had been on the washing line on Saturday when the smoke had drifted everywhere. Still, she didn't have a choice. She'd have to wear it. There was only one week of school term left, and then she could stop thinking about uniforms and washing.

By the time Kirsty had changed she was later than she should have been, so she brushed her hair on the school bus, using the old plastic hairbrush that wasn't half as nice as Fawn's. In the classroom, she and Toby joined the queue for handing in projects.

"Everyone's talking about Georgia and Sally's," she said as they walked back to their desks. "Apparently they've even done a DVD."

"So?" said Toby, sliding into his seat. "It's probably just their cheesy smiling faces, pretending to be TV presenters. They'll be going –" he grinned and put his head on one side – "*Hi, we're Georgia and Sally – that's*

Jolly Jolly Georgia and Silly Soppy Sally – and we're here to tell you all about pollution. What a long word that is, children! And it's not a very nice thing, is it? We don't like pollution, do we?"

Other children began to watch, grinning. Toby took a ruler and held it up to Kirsty like a microphone.

"Tell me, Missus Woman," he said, *"what do you think about pollution? Have you done any polluting today?"*

Kirsty was laughing, then stopped when someone pulled her hair sharply from behind. She whirled round to see Georgia and Sally behind her, and this time they weren't laughing at her. They were glaring like thunder.

"Kirsty Weaver *is* pollution," said Georgia. Then they walked away holding their noses.

Kirsty pretended not to care, but she understood. They weren't going to forgive her for laughing at what Toby had said. It probably didn't make much difference, though, as they'd get at her anyway, whatever she did. At the beginning of morning break she was working out how best to avoid them when Mrs Baines called her to stay behind.

"Sit down, Kirsty," she said. Kirsty sat, feeling a little shaky with anxiety. What was she in trouble for? Smelling of smoke? Yawning? She yawned again just at the thought of it. Mrs Baines sat opposite her, not smiling.

"I haven't looked properly at the projects yet," she said, "but I've had a quick glance through them, and the one you and Toby did looks very impressive."

"Thank you, miss."

"Which surprises me," Mrs Baines went on. "Because I'm afraid your work has been disappointing this term. You've done some very careless homework, and that isn't like you."

Kirsy turned her hot face away and curled her toes in her shoes.

"Sorry, miss," she said.

"I've asked you this before, Kirsty, but I need to ask you again. Is there anything the matter at home?"

Kirsty set her teeth and stared at the table, saying nothing. Mrs Baines leaned across the table to her. "Is anyone at school bothering you?"

Tell, tell, tell, said the voice of every grown-up she had ever known. *If anybody is bothering you, tell an adult you can trust.*

She knew it was true. But another voice was in her head.

If you tell, they will get you, and it will be worse. It was the voice of the school playground, and it was a loud voice.

Kirsty glanced at Mrs Baines and away again. Briefly, she nodded her head. She stifled another yawn. Very kindly, Mrs Baines asked, "Who's bothering you?"

Kirsty said nothing.

"It's better if you tell me now, before Parents' Night tomorrow," said Mrs Baines.

Kirsty stared miserably at her hands in her lap, thinking how dirty her nails were. She thought of Fawn, who always made her feel strong. She decided that she might tell Mrs Baines about Georgia and Sally on Thursday, when it would be the end of term and they wouldn't be able to get at her any more – well, not at this school, anyway. There was a long silence. She wished the bell would ring, or somebody would walk in, or anything would happen to break the silence. But nothing happened, and finally she said, "Please may I go, Miss?"

Mrs Baines sighed. "Go on, then, Kirsty," she said. "And if anything happens, you tell me. Yes?"

"Yes, miss," she said, because she had to.

For most of that day, Kirsty managed to avoid Georgia and Sally. In the last week of term it was always easy to find a teacher who wanted help with something – sorting out cupboards, clearing away old bits of models, that sort of thing. In the library there were whole shelves of books to be put in order, and Kirsty browsed through them in a warm, sunny corner as she worked her way through them.

Alice Through the Looking-Glass – she had a copy of that at home; it was one of her Auntie Sarah books, but she hadn't read it for years. She'd never really understood it, and had forgotten most of it, but she remembered there was something in there about a fawn. She flicked through the pages.

Oh, yes. Here was the scene, and she settled down with it. Alice walked through a forest, a magic forest that made you forget everything. Alice even forgot her own name and what she was. She had met a fawn, and the fawn couldn't remember what it was, either, so they had walked quite comfortably together through the trees, with Alice's arms round the fawn's neck. But as soon as they were out of the forest, the fawn had suddenly remembered that it *was* a fawn, and saw that Alice was a human, so it had run away, and Alice had to go on without it.

Kirsty closed the book. She'd never liked that bit. She had wished that Alice and the fawn could stay together for ever.

She yawned, closing her eyes and feeling the sun from the window falling on her face. She imagined a long walk through the trees with Fawn, just the two of them, with no names, walking through the forest as friends. Fawn talked to her in Auntie Sarah's voice. Then quite suddenly he spoke in a very different voice, a boy's voice. He said, "Kirsty!", and she knew it was all over. The fawn knew her name and his own, and they had left the safe, leafy forest of forgetfulness.

"Kirsty!" Toby was saying. "Wake up!"

"I wasn't asleep," she said, but she knew she had been, and she felt better for it. "I'm just helping with the. . ."

"I can see what you're doing. The bell's gone, didn't you hear it?"

Kirsty jumped to her feet. "I have to go to the loo," she said. "If I'm not in class when Mrs Baines calls the roll, will you tell her I was helping—"

"Yeah, just move!" said Toby. Kirsty hurried to the loo, washed hastily, caught sight of herself in the mirror and was shocked. Had she looked that bad all morning? Anyone would think she hadn't combed her hair for a week. She pulled the brush from her bag and gave a few rough strokes, which would have to do.

The room felt too still. She was being watched.

She looked in the mirror and couldn't see anybody else, but giggles came from somewhere behind her. Georgia and Sally were watching her from the doorway, and Kirsty longed to slap their silly, smirking faces. Georgia tossed her hair dramatically.

"I have to look beautiful for my darling Toby," she simpered.

"My hair is so smooth and glossy!" squeaked Sally, and doubled over laughing.

Kirsty ignored them and walked to the door, expecting them to block her way. *Never hide in corners, Fawn, you could get trapped.* Georgia and Sally drew back, holding their noses and flapping the air as Kirsty walked between them, looking straight ahead.

Sally's foot caught her ankle and she fell sprawling on the floor. With a shriek Sally fell on top of her, and as they both struggled to stand, Georgia pushed Kirsty down again. There was a fast, firm click of heels in the corridor and she looked up to see Mrs Baines.

"Georgia! Sally! Kirsty! In the classroom. Now!"

Kirsty's hairbrush had fallen on the floor. She reached for it, but so did Sally, and Kirsty's nails caught across Sally's arm. Sally cried out.

"Miss, Kirsty scratched me!" she screamed.

"Miss, Kirsty attacked Sally!" wailed Georgia dramatically.

"Please, miss, it was an accident!" cried Kirsty.

"Miss, Kirsty tripped her. . ."

"Ow, miss, ow, it really hurts. . ."

"Classroom. Now!" Mrs Baines didn't shout it. She said it in a low, dangerous voice that made Kirsty think of a leopard. She struggled to her feet, looking for her hairbrush, and was just in time to see Georgia slipping it into her own bag. As Mrs Baines marched the three of them back to the classroom, Sally was rubbing her eyes and sniffing while Georgia kept a protective arm round her and Kirsty followed, pretending not to notice. She spent the afternoon trying to get near enough to Georgia to get her hairbrush back, but Mrs Baines was doing a very good job of keeping them apart. Later, Georgia went meekly to the desk to explain that, please, miss, Kirsty Weaver scratched Sally and please, miss, can we go and wash it in case it gets infected? (*I hope it does*, thought Kirsty grimly, looking at her grubby nails.) Mrs Baines agreed that Sally could go and wash her arm, then added that Sally could go by herself.

"She doesn't need you to hold her hand, Georgia," she said drily.

Finally, school was over. As Kirsty hurried out for the bus, she heard Mrs Baines call her name, and pretended not to hear. She was still hoping to get her hairbrush back. Threats and anger would do no good, so she decided to try being sweet and

189

reasonable instead.

"Georgia," she said calmly when they were outside, "I'd like my hairbrush back, please."

"What do you mean?" asked Georgia innocently. "What hairbrush? Sally, do you know anything about a hairbrush?"

"I don't know anything about a hairbrush," said Sally.

Kirsty wasn't going to make an issue of it. It would only end in more humiliation. If it had been Fawn's hairbrush, the Auntie Sarah hairbrush, she might have put up a fight.

People were starting to watch them. Kirsty turned and walked away, thinking of Fawn, her talisman. Who cared about a hairbrush, or a skirt that smelled of smoke; who cared about school, or silly girls who had nothing to do but tease and bully? She had Fawn. Her baby, her young hart, her talisman, her magic charm. Nothing else mattered. She got on to the bus and sat down next to Toby just in time to see the hairbrush thrown into the road, where a car ran over it. Toby twisted round.

"What was that?" he asked.

Somebody in front of them said, "Hairbrush, I think." Toby turned to look at Kirsty, who shrugged and said nothing.

At home Kirsty found Mum asleep surrounded by sketches, more of them this time. There were yellow and gold buttercups with shine on their petals, sweet peas and dog roses, pink and white. Kirsty picked one up. Dog roses, and the white frail flowers of brambles. Where had Mum seen those dog roses and brambles together? Had she been out on her own, and walked up the hill to draw them?

There was damp grass on Mum's shoes and Kirsty felt the smile grow inside her. Mum had gone out, alone! Her first thought was to run to the garage and share her excitement with Dad – but she'd better not. Dad hadn't seemed very pleased about Mum going out the last time, when she and Kirsty had gone to watch the deer together. Kirsty bent and kissed Mum gently, so as not to wake her up.

"Well done, you brave mum!" she whispered. "Get better!"

She tiptoed out, made Fawn's bottle and collected leaves and grasses. When she went to the shed, Fawn clambered quickly to his feet and ran to her for the milk. He finished it so quickly she was afraid he'd choke on it, then he shook his head and rooted about on the floor for leaves. She reached to put an arm round his neck, but he flinched and ducked away.

"Good boy," she said. "I know I shouldn't hug you, but I just feel like hugging someone."

He ignored her, stepping elegantly past her to inspect more leaves. For a deer who guzzled so furiously at a bottle of milk he was wonderfully dainty with the grasses, tasting and testing and pulling out small mouthfuls at a time. As she sat on a pile of hay, she felt the miserable day fading away from her. Georgia,

Sally, and everything else in the school world were shut out. She was in Fawn's world, watching his velvet soft eyes, the wise, twitching ears, and the pattern of white spots on his warm brown coat. She would never tire of looking at him.

"Let's not grow up," she said quietly. "Don't grow antlers. Don't go round the hill bellowing and fighting. I know I can't keep you here for ever, so I'll come up and live on the hill with you. I'd be cold in winter, and I'd miss Mum. I suppose I'd miss Dad, too, just not his grumpiness. But I'd sort of want him to miss me." She thought a bit longer, twisting a stalk of hay round her fingers. "You know what I'd really love? I'd love to go and work in a place where they look after animals like you. Hurt ones, and lost ones. Rejected ones. Odd ones. Do you think I could work somewhere like that? I'd call it Fawn's House or Fawn Hill, or something, after you."

Yes, that was a nice daydream. One day, it might even happen. In the meantime, she'd have to borrow Fawn's hairbrush.

Outside the garage, Mal was wiping oil from his tattooed hands and growling to Dad – something about "ought to lock them all up and throw away the key" – until Dad saw Kirsty, and hushed him up. That sort of thing happened a lot just now.

"I'll come in presently and do tea," said Dad, so Kirsty went indoors and looked again at Mum's pictures, more carefully this time, picking them up one by one. Among the softly shaded sweet peas and roses, one pencil sketch fell out. It was a sketch of a baby, a very tiny baby, with a creased face and its eyes tightly shut.

"Is that you, Joseph?" whispered Kirsty. "Joseph, is that you? I'm your big sister."

For the second time that day, she felt she was being watched. Mum was awake. She was looking at Kirsty with the drawing in her hand.

"That's my brother, Joseph, isn't it?" said Kirsty.

Mum nodded. "He was beautiful," she said.

"Yes, he was," said Kirsty, and there was no need to say anything else, no need to hug, or cry, or ask questions. Whatever had happened in the past, whatever was happening with the garage, things were getting better for Mum.

"You really are my talisman," Kirsty told Fawn as she settled him down for the night. "Mum's definitely better since you arrived. And I wouldn't be such friends with Toby and his family if not for you. You make things right. I wonder what I did before you came."

Yes, what did I do before he came?

What will I do when he's gone?

The following evening was Parents' Night, so there was only just time to get home, feed Fawn, and eat before Kirsty and Dad went out to school. A reassuring smile from Dad would have been good, but Dad didn't smile much these days. He usually looked as if he was going to growl, or be executed, or both.

"Now, remember," he said as he parked the car at school, "when we're in school, don't discuss any private family business."

"What private family business would I want to discuss?" Kirsty asked. She got out, shut the car door, and dug her hands into the pockets of her hoodie.

"You know perfectly well what," he said grimly.

Did she? There was too much to choose from. Auntie Sarah? Mum? Broken glass and smoking cars at the garage? Dad not wanting her to go to Toby's house? She began to wish that parents had a Children's Night, somewhere you could go with your parents and discuss their behaviour, and hear what sort of marks they'd been getting, and ask them silly questions about whether they were trying hard enough.

He looked at her again as they walked to school.

"I don't remember that hoodie," he remarked.

"I've had it for ages," she said. He didn't look sure, but he didn't argue. She felt pretty sure that he had no idea what sort of top she was supposed to have.

Georgia and Sally must have been in early, because Kirsty and Dad were walking into the hall as they walked out. Their sullen faces were almost comical, and four grim-faced parents followed them like prison guards.

"Not a good report there, then," muttered Dad to Kirsty under his breath. When they came to sit uneasily side by side, facing Mrs Baines across her desk, Kirsty's books lay open in front of them. Kirsty wriggled uncomfortably. She was ashamed of those books. As usual, Mrs Baines started with all the nicest things she could say, while Dad smiled proudly and Kirsty wondered what was coming next.

"However," said Mrs Baines (*that means "but"* thought Kirsty), "we've had some disappointing work from you this term, Kirsty." She pointed out some pages of incorrect maths and straggly handwriting. "This is just careless, very careless, and some of your homework looks as if you've done it in a hurry because you wanted to get it out of the way and watch television. Does she watch a lot of television, Mr Weaver?"

"I can't say she does," said Dad, leaning back in his chair and crossing his legs. "Mind, I sometimes find her watching a movie with her mum."

Kirsty darted a glare of fury at him. *Why do you think I do that?*

But Mrs Baines only went on to say, "And lately Kirsty finds it hard to concentrate in lessons. She looks extremely tired sometimes."

Dad looked down at Kirsty. "What's this about?" he asked. Kirsty sat on her hands and looked at the floor.

"I think I might have a clue about what's going on, though," continued Mrs Baines. Kirsty blushed scarlet. "I have just been speaking to two thoroughly shamefaced bullies who have been picking on Kirsty. I saw them throw a hairbrush into the road yesterday, and I suspect it was yours, Kirsty?"

Kirsty glanced up at her, turned red and hot,

and nodded.

"This has been going on all this term, hasn't it?" persisted Mrs Baines.

"Yes, miss," she whispered.

Mrs Baines sighed. "I wish you'd told me," she said. "I could have put a stop to this sooner." She leaned forward. "Is there anything else?"

Kirsty looked again at her hands in her lap. There was a graze where she'd banged her knuckles on the shed door and scratches from gathering brambles for Fawn. Was there anything else? *My mum's depressed, Dad's grumpy all the time and doesn't want me to tell you anything. Auntie Sarah died, and if you don't think that's important it's because you don't know anything about us and Auntie Sarah. And I have a fawn to look after. But he's not a problem. Keeping him secret and safe is a problem, but he's not. Fawn and I live in our own secret world, and I'm not letting either of you into it.*

"Kirsty?" asked Mrs Baines. "Is there anything?"

Kirsty shook her head. "There's nothing."

Mrs Baines sat back. There clearly *was* something, but Kirsty wasn't going to tell her about it.

"Finally," she said, "I've looked at the project you and Toby have done about wildlife and pollution. Now that, Kirsty, is an excellent piece of work. You and Toby should be very proud of it."

"Thank you, miss," said Kirsty.

Dad looked surprised. "Oh, is that project all finished, then?" he said.

"We handed it in yesterday," said Kirsty.

He seemed to relax after that. He said nothing during the drive home, but when he parked the car he said a bit about what she'd done well and what she'd done badly, and how she should concentrate better, while Kirsty only half-listened. Finally he said, "So now you've finished your project, you can stop going up to Hart Hill Farm."

The words hit Kirsty like a slap in the face. It was as if the house had fallen down around her, and she had fallen with it.

"I don't need to," she said, "but I can still go there, can't I?"

"Not just yet," said Dad. "I don't think you should, not for a while."

"But in the school holidays. . ." she began.

"I said no!" shouted Dad.

Tears were prickling Kirsty's eyes. "But Toby's my best friend!" she cried. "*Why* can't I go there?"

"Kirsty, you know perfectly well!" he growled. "I'm working twenty-four hours a day to keep the garage going, I can't look after your mum as well! We can't risk her wandering off somewhere and getting lost and distressed because you've gone out for the day! I need you to stay here!"

"That's all wrong!" she argued. "Mum's fine when I'm at school, why can't she get on all right in the holidays? It's nearly my school holiday, Dad, and I've been looking forward to – to – just getting out!" She wanted to stop, but she couldn't, now she'd started. "All I want to do is go to my friend's house, just like other people do! It's better than being here, where it's all tyres and cars and everyone's miserable and I have to do all the work!"

"That's enough!" thundered Dad. "Just do as you're told, OK? Just do it, and don't argue."

The unfairness made Kirsty furious. "What are you doing?" she cried. "Do you want to make me a prisoner? You're already doing that to Mum!"

Dad's knuckles were white. He was staring at the steering wheel, and he spoke in a tight, slow voice as if he could only just control his temper.

"I've got enough trouble without you starting," he said. "I don't have to explain everything to you! You stay home after school for the rest of this week. And you're not dashing off places as soon as it's the holidays. And don't ask questions."

Kirsty scrambled out of the car and slammed the door. "I hate you!" she screamed. She ran upstairs, banged her bedroom door, pulled off her shoes and hurled them at the wall. The door opened. Dad was there, giving orders in a harsh whisper.

"Stop that now! Do you want to upset your mum?"

Kirsty hadn't thought she could be angrier. But she could.

"Don't you threaten me like that!" she hissed back at him. "Don't you bully me and then say, 'Oh be quiet, you'll scare Mum'! That is so weak! You're just afraid of what Mum would say to you if she found out that you've stopped me going out! You're using Mum to get at me and that is disgusting! Mum and I would be better without you!"

"Stay in your room!" he ordered, and left, shutting the door firmly behind him. She waited to see if he'd come back. Sooner or later, she needed to go to Fawn. But Dad didn't return, and presently Mum came in.

"Hello, sweetheart," she said. "How was Parents' Night?"

"It was fine," she said. "Mrs Baines really liked my project – I mean, Toby's and mine."

"Good," she said. "Toby seems nice." She looked at Kirsty again. "I don't remember that top."

"It was Tessa Gordon's," said Kirsty, and the voice of her daydream rose inside her saying – *She noticed! Mum noticed!* "Tessa grew out of it, and her mum offered it to me." She spoke just a little too loudly, hoping that Dad would hear, because he wouldn't like it, but he wouldn't be able to do a thing about it. He'd never noticed when she didn't have a proper coat. "It's really comfortable, I love it."

"Did you thank her properly?"

"Course I did, Mum," she said, smiling.

"Will you say thank you to her from me, for the flowers? And the magazines – I enjoyed those."

"Course I will, but you should meet her," suggested Kirsty. "She's lovely." When Mum had gone she waited for the house to grow quiet, then went out to the shed to talk to the only person who made sense.

The warm, animal smell of the shed began to calm and soothe Kirsty the moment the door shut behind her. She gave Fawn his bottle, an apple she'd picked up from the kitchen, and a handful of buttercups and dandelions, then she patted his neck and, because it had all been too much, sat down on the hay for a little cry. *If this were a soppy film*, she thought, *Fawn would come and nuzzle me. But he doesn't, because he knows he's a deer and deer don't do that.* She was proud of that. He still behaved like a deer. She curled up her knees and rested her head on her arms, watching Fawn.

"Dad isn't usually like this," she said. "Mum's getting better; he should be pleased. He's always a bit quiet, he's not one of those fun dads, but he's my dad, and he's usually OK. Now he's just grumpy and snappy. What's wrong with going to see Toby and his family, Fawn? The Gordons don't mind me. And this thing about keeping me and Mum at home, what's that for? I know he's got problems with the garage and everything, but he shouldn't be taking it out on me. I've got problems, lots of them, and I don't take it out on him. He can't just lock us away so he doesn't have to deal with us. Your home shouldn't be a prison." She stretched out her hand towards Fawn, then drew it back again. "Is that what I'm doing to you, Fawn? Am I keeping you a prisoner?"

Fawn wasn't giving her any answers, so she had to think it out for herself. *The police came, and Dad seemed to think that everything was sorted out. Maybe it isn't, not yet. Maybe he isn't.*

"Grown-ups," she said. "What can you do with

them? Fawn, it's getting so complicated here. There are grown-ups behaving badly, and I don't know what they're going to do next. So I need to get you out, as soon as I can. OK?" And she wondered what she would do, all through the long summer holidays, without him. It felt too soon.

Chapter Twelve

For the last few days of term, Georgia and Sally avoided her. They didn't even wrap their arms round each other when Kirsty and Toby were together. Kirsty was pretty certain that this was because they'd had "a word" from Mrs Baines. Toby said it was because they'd had a word from him.

"I told them my dad could get people sent to prison," he said. "Or Young Offenders places. It looks as if it worked."

Kirsty wasn't sure about this, but she was happy with the way it had turned out. But she still couldn't go to Toby's house. She and Toby got an A for their project, and she had run into the house shouting about it, but Dad still wouldn't let her go to Hart Hill after school.

"But he hasn't stopped me coming to see you," Toby

pointed out on the last day of term, "so I can still see You-Know-Who."

"Maybe," she said. "But Dad would probably find some way of banning you from the house. And the garage. And the shed." She managed a little laugh. "He'll be putting up barbed wire next. Electric fences. Searchlights."

Toby only grinned. "He can't stop Mum and Dad stopping at the garage to check their tyres," he said.

"Perhaps he'll change," said Kirsty. "I hope so. All those things happening at the garage, it's getting to him, but he won't talk about it – except to Mal, and Mal won't tell me anything. Dad's been worse since that car caught fire. And maybe he's got a good reason; maybe they're still threatening him. Do you think those men might come back and do something worse? What are we going to do?"

Toby had no answer. She could almost hear him trying to think of one, but there was only a long silence. *A loud silence*, she thought miserably.

"Think of something, to keep Fawn safe," she said at last.

"Could we move him into our lambing shed?" was all he could come up with. They talked about how to get him across the road and up there in secret, and what to do if he bolted, but they didn't come up with any answers. All they could do was agree to go on thinking about it.

"And keep a close eye on the shed," suggested Toby. "Look out for anything suspicious."

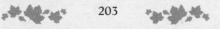

203

That evening, Kirsty stayed for a long time in the shed with Fawn. Watching his wide-eyed young face, she thought that he was too young to go back to the hill yet. He was still only a baby. But the other young deer on the hill had that delicate, vulnerable look about them, and they all seemed to be thriving. He was growing taller all the time, and had filled out.

But those growing muscles needed to be strong, too, to give him a chance of survival. He needed exercise, and that meant leaping and racing without the confined walls of the shed. He had to be able to find his own food, and to drink water from the running stream like the deer in the herd, not from a bowl filled up from the outside tap. As if he had read her thoughts, he began to run.

"No more school for six weeks!" she said. "Freedom! Fawn, you don't know how good the sunshine feels, or what the grass smells like when it's been raining. You should have all that. You're not a baby, but you're not grown up, either. If you were free, would you cope? Would you be all right if I let you out. . ." She had meant to say "now", but she couldn't, so instead she said "soon", then changed it to "soonish". She waited until he had stopped running and jumping ("and kicking dust in my face, thank you"), and got up to go.

At the door, she stopped. *You beautiful, beautiful fawn*, she thought. And her heart warmed with the thought that, for all these weeks, she had lived so close to a creature like this.

"Thanks for putting up with me, Fawn," she said.

"What would you like tomorrow? Carrot? Rose petals?" And yet again, though she felt she shouldn't, she patted his neck. "Beautiful," she said again.

Kirsty went back to the house, put her school things in the wash (*won't have to think about these again!*), showered, and kissed goodnight to Auntie Sarah's picture, but she didn't go to bed. *Keep a close eye on the shed*, Toby had said. Wrapped in her dressing gown, she sat up on her bed, ready for any whiff of smoke, or sounds of a car approaching. When Mum and Dad went to bed, she crept downstairs to watch from the windows.

Nothing happened. Time passed. She became bored, and cold, and her eyes were closing. Her mind drifted into sleep, and at last she slipped silently upstairs to bed, determined to wake early in the morning, but, of course, she didn't. She slept late, and was woken by the sound of voices in the forecourt. Whatever time it was, work at the garage had begun.

The day was breezy and warm, a perfect first day of the school holidays, and the bottle she had made up was still too hot to give to Fawn. She put it in her pocket and walked a little way up the hill to pull up leaves and dandelions for him, and gradually forgot about tiredness, and worry, and danger, and everything except him, until the bottle was cool enough and she turned back downhill to the shed.

He had heard her. Already he was trotting towards her, raising his head and sniffing the air. She had to shut the door quickly to keep him in.

"I know, I know," she said. "Yes, my beautiful boy, it

205

does smell good out there. You want to be on the hill. But just for now, you need. . ."

She laughed. He was butting her gently, seeking his bottle. He sucked at it, but not as hard as he used to, and he seemed more interested in chewing the fresh dandelions. Outside a car pulled up, but he ignored it and went on eating.

"You're supposed to be afraid of traffic," she said. "I suppose that's a problem with keeping you here." She watched him, knowing that even if she kept him for ever she would never tire of his gentle eyes, his delicate face, his graceful shape. She knew every white spot on his back, every shade of his coat, every eyelash.

"You are the most amazing thing that ever happened to me," she said. "And when you're a grown-up hart on the hill, I'll come up there and look at you and think *He's mine!* even though you can never really belong to anyone. I'll always think of you, but you won't think of me. No, don't flick your ears at me like that, because you won't. You have to forget me." She mustn't go on thinking like that, so she thought of something sensible instead. "You need fresh water," she said.

Tap. Tap. Tap.

Knuckles rapped against the shed door. Fawn bolted into a stall. Kirsty turned cold.

"It's only me," whispered a voice.

"Toby!" She opened the door quickly and ushered him in. The sudden shock and fear made her angry. "Why didn't you say so, instead of tapping like a ghost? I was terrified! Fawn bolted!"

"There's no need to go off on one. I persuaded Mum that she needed some windscreen stuff and her tyres checking," he said. "She's in the garage with Tessa and your dad."

"Tessa's here?"

"Mum's dropping her off at the stables. I planned that neatly, didn't I?"

"You're a cleverclogs," she said, but she no longer felt angry. "I was just going to get him some. . ."

She never did tell him what she was going to get. Outside, brakes squealed painfully. With the screech came a smell of hot rubber that made her remember the fire so vividly that she felt sick. Car doors banged. Men's voices were shouting.

"Morning, Weaver!" yelled someone.

"Good morning, Andy? Busy today?"

"We've got some business for you, Andy!"

Kirsty and Toby looked at each other without speaking. It was like hearing Georgia and Sarah again, but far worse. These voices were male, adult, and brutal. And they were very close.

"Morning, Weaver Beaver! We've come to pay you a visit!"

"We promised!"

"We've got something for you!"

"It's them! Blondie and Rat!" whispered Kirsty.

There was a ringing clang of metal. A sickening smash of glass. Even in the stable, Kirsty ducked. Then something banged three times against the door of the shed. She edged towards the stall where Fawn crouched, alert and watchful, his ears twitching.

"Quiet now," she soothed him, but her hand shook. "You're all right. Keep still for me. Good Fawn!"

From outside came a *crack-bang!* like a firework and Toby ducked, too.

"Gunshot!" he whispered.

Another bang. A man's voice cried out. Toby reached for the door.

"Don't!" gasped Kirsty. "Stay here! Have you got your phone?"

"My mum and Tessa are out there," said Toby, and threw her his phone. "You get the police, I'm going out."

If Toby was going out, so was she. She couldn't protect Fawn if she didn't know what was going on. She was tapping three nines into the phone as she slipped out of the shed, pushing the door shut behind her and pressing her back against it to keep it closed.

The blond man was sprawled on the ground in the middle of the forecourt with Mal kneeling on top of him, holding on to his wrist. A long, thin gun lay on the ground, but there was only a second to take this in as the other man, the rat-haired man, ran furiously towards the shed, lifting a cricket bat in both hands.

Toby stuck out his foot. With a shout, the man stumbled and fell in front of her, still holding the cricket bat. Then Toby was on top of him, Tessa and Mrs Gordon were running towards them – but the man was too strong for Toby. He had thrown him off, he was raising the bat—

Kirsty leapt forward and kicked the raised arm with all her strength. The bat flew from the man's fist and over the fence. She sprang back to her place at the stable door, but she was too late. It flew open, knocking her to the ground as Fawn leapt out, swerved round them, galloped to the fence and cleared it. Mrs Gordon was running to help them.

"Sit on his legs, Toby!" yelled Mrs Gordon, and pinned the man's arms to the ground.

Kirsty struggled to her feet, her eyes on Fawn. He stood on the other side of the fence, watching her as he sniffed the air. At a shout and a barrage of foul language from the man on the ground he darted away, keeping at a safe distance. Kirsty, getting her breath, shaking a little, walked slowly towards him. He needed to be calmed.

"Hush now," she said. "You're all right. Hush." She gazed at him. That gentle face, with the huge dark eyes. His graceful shape. Softly, she asked, "What are you going to do, Fawn?"

He looked back at her, then turned, flicked his ears and raised his head to smell the air of the hill and the woods. Clover. Dandelion. Roses. Grasses. Leaves. He scented all the good things she had ever brought him. He felt soft damp grass under his hooves and the wideness of the space. Memory stirred in his head, and it was good. He turned, trotted up the path, and suddenly broke into a joy of running, skipping and swerving, ignoring the path, bounding away through the grass and into the trees, out of sight.

"Well done," she whispered, but she could feel the emptiness of the shed behind her like a gap in her

209

heart. She turned, rubbing a few tears from her eyes, as a siren wailed along the road.

As the police arrived, Kirsty sat on the fence and watched the scene. The battered blue car was parked at an angle outside the garage, the doors wide open. Police officers were handcuffing the two men, pulling them to their feet and bundling them into police cars, and one officer – the one she had seen last time they came – stayed to take statements from everyone. Mrs Gordon came to stand beside her.

"Kirsty, are you all right?" she asked.

Kirsty looked back up the hill, where Fawn had gone. For a moment she wanted to hug Mrs Gordon, but that wouldn't be right, not with Mum standing outside looking bewildered. In the forecourt, everyone seemed to be talking too fast, too loudly, and all at once.

". . .are you all right?"

". . .scared the daylight out of me. . ."

". . .good rugby tackle, Mal!"

". . .only an air gun. . ."

"Blanks? Were they blanks?"

"Debbie! Debbie, it's all right. . ."

"Where did that deer come from?"

". . .what deer?"

". . .deer . . . Kirsty . . . Toby . . . Debbie . . . deer . . . gun . . . broken . . . hurt . . . gun. . ."

It was too much, the noise, the confusion, the fuss. Kirsty turned and ran up the hill. Voices shouted after her, calling her back, but above them she heard Toby calling, "Just let her go, you have to let her go!" and Mal, as ever, saying what was so obvious:

"Leave her be. She'll come back when she's ready."

Kirsty found the place where she had first seen Fawn and sat there, screened from the deer. It was much warmer now than it had been then, and by the time she reached this place she knew exactly why she had to be here.

Too much had happened at once. She couldn't cope with everything at the same time, all that had happened at home and Fawn's escape as well. The others could sort out blue cars, thugs and air guns. Fawn had run to a place he knew to be his sanctuary, the green world that would shelter him, and she had done the same. It was a healing place. She sat down to watch, hoping to see him. She needed to know whether he could cope.

As the morning passed and the sunlight grew stronger, the deer moved more deeply into the shelter of the trees. From time to time a doe would step out, elegant as a lady in high heels, and a fawn would peep from the long grass and run to suckle.

The sun rose higher, and Kirsty shaded her eyes as she watched. Now and again something would move, but it would only be the grass stirring in a breeze, the movement of a bird, or a rabbit running to a burrow.

Something far away seemed to move. The sun was high, and Kirsty had to shelter her eyes and squint. Yes, it was a deer, a small one, coming nearer, and Kirsty sat up straight to watch – but it wasn't him, and she felt

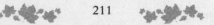

cross with herself. How could she have imagined this fawn to be him? It was nothing like—

She gasped. Something to the right caught her eye. She bit her lip to keep quiet.

He walked with his head down, sniffing at the grasses, stopping to pull up some buttercups, then raising his head and walking on. When he came to the stream he reached down to examine it, looked at it as if making up his mind, then drank. At last, he lifted his wet face and stepped through the stream to join the herd on the other side. In a patch of sunlight he folded his forelegs and lay down as if his whole life had been on this hill.

From the first day, it had been all she had ever wanted for him. A smile of joy and pride spread across her face.

"Well done, my lovely Fawn," Kirsty said. Then she thought of the empty stable and her old coat lying in the hay, and she put her head on her arms and cried.

When she had finished, she felt very peaceful. This was a good place to be, a good, quiet place, with the fresh clear air that smelled of summer and greenness. Fawn seemed quite content. It occurred to her that she would never again stroke his soft neck, or feel him push at her for his bottle, but she had learned to live without Auntie Sarah and she would learn to live without Fawn, too. After all, Fawn was still alive. He wasn't hers. But then, he never had been.

The sky clouded over. Kirsty was feeling thirsty by the time Toby came and sat down beside her.

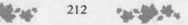

"Is he all right?" asked Toby.

She pointed. Toby tried to follow the line of her finger.

"Which one is he?" he asked. It seemed impossible that he couldn't tell, but, of course, he'd never been as close to him as she had.

"Look along my arm," she said. "Straight along. There are three silver birch trees in a row. Look between the second and third. He's lying down." She paused, then asked, "Do you think he'll be all right?"

"We'll have to keep checking on him," said Toby.

"Yes," she said, smiling. "We will. He just found his own food and drank from the stream, so I think he can look after himself, but you're right. We have to come up and watch him."

"You coming down now?" he asked.

Was she? She didn't want to face them all. It was better up here, with only the deer herd.

"What's it like at home?" she asked. "What are they saying?"

"Um. . ." He seemed to be wondering what to tell her, and she wondered how bad it could be.

"Did anyone get hurt? Am I in trouble?"

"Wait a minute, I'm trying to get things in the right order. OK. Right, now, those two men in the blue car, they're the ones who've been causing all that trouble for your dad because he got the police on to them after they drove off without paying."

"I knew it was them," said Kirsty. "I bet they were the ones who killed Fawn's mother, too."

213

"You don't know that," he said. "You never will; there's no evidence. The police couldn't even get enough evidence for the other things, the graffiti and that, so they couldn't charge them until now, not even when they set fire to the old car."

"I wish Dad had talked to me," she said.

"He was trying to do the right thing, and protect you," said Toby. "By the end they were threatening him that it was going to get a lot worse, and he was scared for you. He reckoned they were going to attack you, or your mum, so he didn't want you out of his sight. He didn't tell you all that because he didn't want you to worry."

"Worry!" she cried. "Of course I worried!"

"Be quiet, you'll frighten the deer. So the blue car men came today just planning to be scary. They said they didn't mean to hurt anyone."

"Why did they. . .?" she began, then remembered to keep her voice down. "Why did they have a gun and a cricket bat if they didn't mean to hurt anyone?"

"They only meant to scare us and make a noise, banging the bat on the shed and firing the gun into the air. Then Mal got the man with the gun in a flying tackle; that's what the yell was about. Your dad had a direct line to the police, your mum was phoning them, so was my mum, and Tessa, and they were taking photos on the phones at the same time."

"Photos?"

"Evidence, silly. So they'll be charged this time, and they know they don't stand a chance of getting off." There was a pause, and then he added, "Are you coming back down yet?" When she said nothing, he went on, "Your dad's really worried about you. Now he's settled down a bit, he says he should have let you come to our house more. . ."

"*More?*"

"Yeah, cos then you would have been safely out of the way, but he just wasn't thinking straight."

Parents! thought Kirsty. She still wasn't sure if she wanted to face them yet, but she'd have to do it sooner or later. "What did they say about Fawn?"

Toby shrugged. "Not much," he said.

"What!" She was so astonished she forgot to be quiet, and the deer all turned their heads. Toby jabbed his elbow into her arm to keep her quiet. "*Not much?*"

"They said, 'Where did that deer come from?'" he admitted. "I mean, there's guns and cricket bats and rugby tackles and sirens and everyone falling over and yelling, and all that. It was a while before they got as far as talking about the deer, and then my mum said to me, 'Do you know anything about that?'"

"What did you say?" asked Kirsty.

Toby frowned as if this were a difficult maths problem. "I said yes, I did know about it," he explained. "But I said I'd made a promise not to say anything. But I couldn't stop them going to look at the shed, so I think they've pretty much worked it out. I told them that everything you did was good."

"Thanks," she said, and finally added, "I suppose we should go down now."

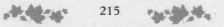

215

"Yes, we should," said Toby, getting up. "Are you hungry? Cos I am."

"Sorry," she said. She should have thought of that. She got up and brushed herself down, but as they walked away she glanced back over her shoulder, and smiled.

"Oh, come on," said Toby, "you can see him again later."

The look had been for Fawn, but the smile wasn't. The smile was because she knew she had a great friend, a friend like herself, who wasn't a fawn.

Chapter Thirteen

On an August day near the end of the holidays, Kirsty climbed the hill again to sit in her favourite spot and check that Fawn was still happy. She did this every day, but today, near the end of the holidays, she wanted to look back.

To her surprise, nobody had been angry with her for sheltering Fawn. They had said she was silly, and that she should have told an adult and they would have brought in the RSPCA, or a vet. They insisted that nobody would have shot him or turned him into venison. Dad pointed out that Fawn could have become ill and died in those long hours when he had been alone and she was at school. Kirsty had cried because she realized that this was true, and then Mum had said very firmly that it wasn't Kirsty's fault if she didn't have a grown-up she could talk to. Then Mum had cried too, and Dad had said it was like sitting with a lot of women at a weepie movie. Then he'd walked away in a hurry and Kirsty guessed that he was crying, too, and she had laughed and cried at the same time.

That first night, they left the shed door open in case Fawn came back. He didn't, but he came to the fence the next day, and for two more days after that. The first day, Kirsty had run to make up a bottle, but by the time she brought it, he had disappeared. The next day, he took some grass from her hand. The next, he did not, and he never came down the hill again.

Mum was definitely getting better. She was seeing a doctor and a psychologist. The life came back into her eyes. One morning she came downstairs saying she was sick to death of this dim grim house, and it needed sorting. Within a week they had cleaned, dusted, painted all the walls in light colours, thrown out bin bags full of clutter, washed everything washable, and changed all the curtains except Kirsty's. Mum and Toby's mum would get together for coffee. They'd take carloads of old clothes to the charity shop because Mum wanted a fresh start. Then they'd make a trip or two into town to buy new clothes and get Mum's hair done. Mum looked new.

Mum took Kirsty into town, too, to buy her new school uniform, shoes, a hairbrush, and a coat, a quilted one, ready for the winter. It looked so shop-window perfect that Kirsty thought she'd never dare wear it. Then they'd gone to a cafe for milkshakes and chocolate brownies, and laughed a lot, and now and again Kirsty kicked herself under the table to make sure she wasn't dreaming.

Day by day, Kirsty learned to live with the gap in her life where Fawn had been. It made her think of Mum, and the death of little Joseph. That wasn't like a much-loved fawn going out to a life in the wild. That was a treasured baby who would never be alive, never open his eyes to see the person who loved him best. No wonder Mum found it so hard.

Dad had been worried about Kirsty having friends who were "something to do with the law". But he found out that these people who were something to do with the law were happy to help with things that bothered him, like VAT, and late payments. In fact, they all got to be friends with Toby's family. Kirsty even went out riding with Tessa. Some of Tessa's friends were a bit snobby, but Tessa herself was all right. In September Kirsty would go to the comprehensive and Toby would make the long journey to a school in town every day, but they knew it wouldn't matter too much. They'd still be friends.

When Mum had finished painting the house she got out her pastels and watercolours, her easel and brushes, and went back to painting flowers. Some of her pictures went up in the house, and soon some were for sale in art shops in town. She made packets of gift cards to sell, too. The garage shop was cleaned up, ready to open again, but Mum hadn't made up her mind whether to run it herself or employ somebody else and concentrate on her painting. Kirsty didn't mind much what Mum did, so long as she was well. It seemed as if Fawn, her talisman, her hart, had made it all happen.

And the shed?

Once it was quite clear that Fawn wasn't coming back, they had all swept and cleaned the shed and scrubbed it out until the only trace of Fawn was a carefully wrapped tissue of deer hairs, treasured with the Auntie Sarah things. It was as if he had never lived in the shed at all. Then Mrs Gordon and Tessa came to see Kirsty, and brought her an envelope.

"We took photographs on our phones of the attack on the garage," said Mrs Gordon. "The police had to go through them first, but then we put them on the computer. We thought you'd like these ones."

Kirsty opened the envelope Mrs Gordon handed her, aware of them watching her. She drew out the photographs, and a smile spread against her face.

The man on the ground, Toby and Kirsty struggling with him, and a blurry Fawn running past them. Fawn clearing the fence. And one more, clearer this time. Fawn on the wooded side of the fence as Kirsty faced him and waited to see what he would do.

It brought back frightening memories of that day. But, more importantly, it was Fawn. She slipped the precious pictures back into their envelope and looked up with shining eyes.

"Thank you," she said.

*

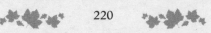

220

Now that the house was clean, decorated, and bright again, it was a shock for Kirsty to go into her bedroom and see a battered, dusty suitcase and a cobwebby cardboard box on the floor. She was about to run downstairs and ask what they were doing in her room when she saw her name scrawled on them in felt pen. Dad looked dusty and cobwebby too, as he explained.

"We thought it was time we got Sarah's stuff out of the loft," he said. "We didn't have the heart to do it before. There's some stuff for your mum, and those boxes are for you. I reckon it's books and stuff." Kirsty was grateful to him for going away and leaving her alone to look through it.

There were wildlife magazines that Auntie Sarah must have collected for years. More books. Some pretty scarves and gloves, and a necklace. *It's like Christmas*, thought Kirsty. She shook out a scarf and an envelope fell from it like an autumn leaf. Her name was on the front in a spidery version of Auntie Sarah's handwriting, and she opened it.

Dear Kirsty,

I hope you can read my writing! My hands don't always do what they're supposed to do just now.

Dearest Kirsty, I'm not going to get better, and there are things I want you to know before I get all dozy and mixed up. I can't write much, and I won't waste time telling you to live a good life, and be happy, and be kind and be true to yourself and so on, because you know all that. We both know that you'll always look out for creatures that can't look out for themselves – humans and animals. So here are some things you might not know—

1. You can have a great life without me.

2. I love you forever, dying doesn't make any difference to that.

3. You are a STAR, STAR, STAR. Really, Kirsty. I don't think you know how much joy you've brought to my life. You've been my niece, my friend, my nearly daughter, my bright light, the one who makes me laugh and makes me feel very special. My Kirsty.

Hugs
Sarah

Kirsty read it over and over, and held it close as if she could press it right into her heart. So she had meant all that to Auntie Sarah. She felt taller, stronger, and more alive than ever in her life before.

They still hadn't decided what to do with the shed, but they all felt it should be used for something. Dad had suggested making it into a gallery where Mum and other artists could sell pictures, but Mum didn't think people would go to a garage to look at flower pictures, even if it was on the main road. Tessa said that lots of her pony friends needed to rent stables in the winter. Then one day Mrs Gordon told Kirsty, Toby and Tessa that she was planning a treat for them, and Kirsty had to be ready early the next morning.

"If you're so keen on looking after animals," said Mrs Gordon, "you may as well see how it's done. Kirsty, you'll need your wellies."

They drove through rolling countryside, past signposts pointing to castles, stately homes and parks. The roads became narrower and quieter. They passed isolated farms, then turned along a narrow lane and saw a painted sign decorated with pictures of a deer, a fox, and a swan around the words:

SPINNEY RISE WILDLIFE CARE

"This place isn't usually open to the public," said Mrs Gordon as they got out of the car. "It's a wildlife centre where they care for any wildlife that need them – anything abandoned, sick or injured. They only have open days now and again, but I phoned and they said we could come here today. Wellies on, everyone."

A tall woman in jeans, muddy boots and a sweatshirt with a picture of a fox was walking towards them. She carried a bucket in one hand.

"Tessa, Toby, Kirsty, is that right?" she said. "I'm Izzy; I work here. I'll just feed the foxes, and then you might like to help me with weighing the hedgehogs."

Kirsty supposed that this meant three or four hedgehogs. In fact, there was a room about half the size of their shed, clean as a surgery, with neat rows of the kind of boxes people use to take animals to the vet.

"The idea of Spinney Rise," she said, lifting a sleepy hedgehog out of a box, "is that if a wild animal needs rescue or care, we look after it. If it's injured or ill, we do what we can. Mostly we release them into the wild, but if they're not well enough to survive there, we keep them here. They're safe here, and it's as near to nature as it can be, without the dangers."

"Do you have any deer?" asked Kirsty.

"Oh, yes," said Izzy. "The last one came when it had got its antlers caught in a bush. And sometimes they try to jump fences that are too high for them and get hurt. If they're a bit lame, they can't run fast enough to be safe in the wild, so they stay here in our paddock. Hedgehogs and birds are the worst; we get dozens of them. We started with just one otter."

There was so much more happening at Spinney Rise. In a small, cosy room, two animals that looked like very small puppies lay wrapped in towels. "They're orphan fox cubs, ten days old," said Izzy before feeding them with bottles so tiny they could have been made for dolls. There were deer in the spinney, otters in the stream, and birds with broken wings in the aviary.

"How do you keep going?" asked Kirsty. "Where does the money come from?"

"Donations," said Izzy. "People give us money and do fund-raising things, and a lot of the staff are volunteers. Sorry I can't show you the badgers, they're asleep, but do you want to see the swans?"

They stayed all day at the sanctuary. Kirsty thought of Fawn as she helped Izzy to chop fruit and wash feeding bowls. By the time they had to go home, she had gathered together the courage to ask what she desperately wanted to know.

"How old do you have to be to help here?"

"Older than you," said Izzy, "but not much."

"Oh," said Kirsty.

"What about collecting things?" asked Tessa. "Towels and blankets and stuff?"

"What we do need," said Izzy, "is support from schools to raise money for us. Put up posters, and, as you said, collect towels and things that we need. We can come into schools and do talks, too. We usually take a hedgehog."

"Cool!" said Toby. For the first time, Kirsty thought going to a different school from Toby seemed like a good idea. They could each run a support group. She couldn't help with rearing fawns, but she could raise money for them. Mum could do a picture to sell.

"The other thing we really need is space," said Izzy. "We need places, not too far away, where we can keep hedgehogs. There's never enough room here. And a halfway house for animals before they go into the wild."

Toby and Kirsty looked at each other with hope in their eyes.

"I think. . ." began Kirsty.

"Just ask your mum and dad first this time, Kirsty," said Mrs Gordon.

"So," said Kirsty, sitting on a log in the clearing. "We're going to have more animals in the shed." (There was no sign of Fawn, but she hoped to see him, and talked to him as if he were there.) "Dad says we have to work together on this, and that's fine with me. He says this family should talk to each other more. I think we should listen to each other more, but we're better than we were. I'm going to raise money for Spinney Rise, and when I'm a bit older I can help there, and you remember your old shed? It's going to be a foster home for hedgehogs and things. And, Fawn, I'm sorry. The more I learn about what they do at Spinney Rise, the more I'm amazed that you survived with me looking after you. Still, I did what I could."

As she spoke, a young male deer broke from the cover of the trees. He stood against the skyline, his head raised. She saw the well-known pattern of his white spots, and the little rise on his head where his antlers would grow. Slowly, she stood up.

"Fawn!" she said softly. "Hart! My talisman for ever!"

She thought of the first day, when she had found him crying on the hill because his mother had not come. She had made a promise to that dead mother, and she had kept it, but it wasn't herself she felt proud of. She saw Fawn turn, sniff the air, and walk away from her, slowly, as if he owned the hill.

"Well done, you," she said.

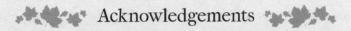 Acknowledgements

I learned a lot about wildlife while working on this book, and the more I learned the more I admired the people who get wet, dirty, tired and bitten rescuing wild animals and caring for them. Very special thanks go to:

Les Stocker and everyone at Tiggywinkles
www.sttiggywinkles.co.uk

Folly Wildlife Rescue
www.follywildliferescue.co.uk

British Wildlife Rescue
British Wildlife Centre
www.britishwildlifecentre.co.uk

Margi comes from Northumberland, is married to a minister, and has three grown-up children. Margi has always loved storytelling and she is the author of the award-winning animal fantasy series, *The Mistmantle Chronicles*. She is also the author of the *Hammy the Wonder Hamster* books, which she wrote as Poppy Harris. Margi loves stories, theatre, gardens, wildlife, history, woodlands and warm fires on winter nights.

www.margaretmcallister.co.uk

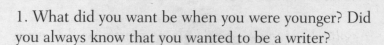

1. What did you want be when you were younger? Did you always know that you wanted to be a writer?

Yes, I did, but at various stages I also wanted to be a dancer (no chance) or an actress. If you're the sort of person who can't see a blank sheet of paper without wanting to write a story on it, you want to be a writer. You can't help it!

2. Where is your favourite place to write?

For the first hand-written draft I can write anywhere, on trains, in the garden, anywhere, but my favourite place is my dining room table. When I'm typing things up, I hide in my attic study with the computer.

3. What were your favourite books and who were your favourite authors when you were younger?

I loved, loved the CS Lewis Chronicles of Narnia *and also the* Green Knowe *books by Lucy Boston. Oh, and Noel Streatfield. Like a lot of female writers I read the* Little Women *series by Louisa May Alcott and was inspired by Jo March, the writer in the family.*

4. Wildlife is very important to Kirsty. Is this something you care about as well? Do you have a favourite animal?

Absolutely. Humans should always remember that we're not the only creatures on the planet. My favourite animal is the red squirrel. They are clever, agile, and so beautiful to watch.

5. Kirsty likes to go to the hill to get some peace and quiet. Is there anywhere in particular that you like to escape to?

My favourite "escape" places – apart from my bed! are (a) my garden and (b) any long, quiet beach. Alnmouth in Northumberland is a favourite.

Useful Websites

As Kirsty discovers, she was very lucky that Fawn survived in her care.

If you find a wild animal in need of help, watch it for a short while to find out how badly hurt it really is. Then contact the RSPCA on 0300 1234 999 and be ready to provide details of the animal and its precise location. Alternatively find a vet or wildlife rehabilitator near you. Do NOT attempt to feed or give water to any injured animal.

Look at these useful websites for more information on how to care for animals:

www.rspca.org.uk
www.scottishspca.org
www.pdsa.org.uk
www.sttiggywinkles.co.uk

If, like Kirsty, you have problems at school, or at home, don't be afraid to tell an adult and ask for help. Here are some useful phone numbers and websites:

Childline 0800 1111 or www.childline.org.uk
Kidscape www.kidscape.org.uk
Young carers www.youngcarers.net

Look out for

A HOME FOR
TEASEL

by Margi McAllister

Coming Soon!